Liberty Gulch
Part One

A.G. Fredericks

ISBN-13: 978-1478387640
ISBN-10: 1478387645

DEDICATION

This book is dedicated to those who work hard, provide for their families, do not assume large amounts of debt, and prepare for whatever the future may hold.

CONTENTS

ACKNOWLEDGMENTS

I would like to thank my patient wife for allowing her husband the necessary hours it takes to write multiple novels while building a budding career as an author. I would also like to thank my editors, Shelly and Doc Trainor for their assistance and attention to detail, without which most of my readers would think I had failed 5th grade English and Grammar.

THE MIDDLE

CHAPTER ONE

Nights were darker ever since the snowstorm took down the power lines. In the past, the lines would have been mended in days and power restored. But not anymore. It was approaching springtime, but the sleeping hours were still cold and we all huddled in front of the fireplace. The upstairs bedrooms had been vacated for months, as far as sleeping was concerned.

The fireplace was always lit, along with some candles around the room as we tried to provide some form of constant light and normalcy. But we had no idea how long our candle supply would last, so we tried our best to use them sparingly.

"Play the guitar, Daddy," Anna gleefully requested.

It was difficult to maintain a light mood in the face of what had happened over the past year. But, at only eight years old, Anna hadn't the frame of reference for what we were beginning to regard as "the good old days." Of her years on the planet, the first seven were spent under what we would have considered "normal" circumstances. But this past year was one of turmoil and devastation, and she had grown somewhat accustomed to her new life and could still maintain a childish joy despite the new hardships. Those who remembered the past more fondly had a tougher time.

Playing the guitar had been a hobby of mine years ago, but now I could only remember a few songs. Even though I always had a good ear for music, I hardly had time during the day to sit down and learn anything new. As such, each night was pretty much the same setlist.

In the beginning, it was only I who would sing. I knew my voice wasn't the prettiest and I'm generally reserved when it comes to such things, but this felt different because it was for Anna. Besides, I was the only one who knew all the words. So I did it, and in the following days the embarrassment was defeated; everyone learned the words and all joined in.

In time, we all fell into our roles. Mitch, one of our house guests, would spend those hours at the upstairs window taking his turn at the guard's post. I sat on the sofa, focusing on the guitar while Foggdog, our other house guest, sat in the chair clapping and singing along in his own way. Charlotte's voice was that of an angel. I never knew until recently that my wife of ten years could sing so well, but when it was quiet and I played low, everyone else would hush up and give her the floor because her voice was the sweetest sound we'd heard in months.

Then there was Anna. Little Anna danced her heart out bringing smiles to our faces that otherwise would have likely never come. At first, she would flail her arms and spin around, often falling and making us laugh in the process. But then, on a trip to the library she asked if she could get a book about dancing. So she did. In fact, she found eight of them.

During the day, she sucked the information right out of those books. She was only eight, but her reading skills were very advanced for her age and she would spend hours in her room (or in the yard if it was warm enough) practicing her heart out. Even though a lot of the songs I knew were not necessarily conducive to dancing, she began to choreograph her own routines to them.

Most importantly, it made her happy. And her happiness was contagious; it gave us the ability to be happy in those moments too, even though there seemed little reason to be.

Foggdog sat in the chair with his legs draped over the side. His mind seemed elsewhere this evening, probably because he hadn't seen his girlfriend in a couple of days due to the heavy rains. Charlotte entered the room with a log in each hand and added them to the fire, which sparkled and roared in response. She then sat next to me as Anna handed me the guitar and I began to play.

The song was *"Rain King"* by the Counting Crows, which I tried to play at a quick pace to make it more conducive to dancing. Charlotte sang her heart out, and livened up the lyrics as Anna danced in the firelight, her brown ponytail whipping around and her steps always more refined than before from all of that practice.

The lyrics were sometimes a reminder of the world we now lived in. "Well, I can't go outside; I'm scared; I might not make it home." With the quick tempo and Charlotte's beautiful voice, I'm not sure that Anna ever caught the meaning of those words, though they were not lost on me. Perhaps this was just the way it was going to be from now on.

Foggdog looked to be nodding off in the chair, which was probably a good thing since he had the early morning watch. Charlotte smiled as she sang, and we watched Anna escape the pains of this new life that she hardly seemed to know.

Things were different; that's for sure. But, in a moment we'd find out just how different they really were.

Mitch's voice called from the guard's post upstairs, "Someone is coming up the hill!"

Charlotte stopped singing in mid-phrase. The last note carried for a momentary second before I deadened the strings. Anna kept dancing away until we hushed her down. Foggdog rose from the chair.

Though we always posted a guard at night, we didn't have a protocol for such an event. Immediately regretting our unpreparedness, I had to jump into action and do something. My instinct was to get up and blow out the candles. So I did. In retrospect, I guess that didn't matter. The fireplace was roaring and there was no time to put it out before the trespasser made his way to the door, so blowing out the candles only served to make the room a little darker.

I struggled to figure out where Charlotte and Anna should hide – the upstairs bedrooms, the basement, or maybe even the backyard? In the end, it didn't matter what I thought because Charlotte grabbed Anna's hand and the two quickly ran upstairs. There was no time to debate whether or not that was the right move and I was at least glad for Charlotte's decisiveness.

"What did you see?" I asked Mitch as he ran down the stairs.

"I don't really know," he answered as he reached the bottom stair. "It's pitch black out there and the rain makes it too difficult to see. But there was definitely a man walking up the road. It was definitely a man."

Mitch held the only gun we had in his hand.

"That thing loaded?" I asked.

"Hell, yeah."

In all the months since we had posted a guard, we had never actually seen anyone near the house. I don't know what I was expecting, but as we sat there arguing over what we should do next, the most unexpected thing happened: the doorbell rang.

Who the hell would ring the doorbell at this hour after walking up the hill in the rain?

Foggdog hung back as Mitch held the gun near the front door. I looked at him to make sure he was ready, and he nodded. Taking a deep breath, I gripped the knob and gave it a quick turn.

It took a moment for me to place him, and even when I did I wasn't quite sure. I had last seen the man about nine months ago, but his sunken eyes and gaunt face made him look about twenty years older. He sported a beard that, like his hair, was wildly unkempt and he looked to have lost about thirty pounds. Sopping wet and exhausted, Art Brady collapsed through the threshold of our door. Somehow I was able to catch his limp body just before it hit the floor.

"It's okay," I said as I looked at Mitch. "I know him. He's a friend."

With that, Mitch put down the gun down and the three of us lifted the visitor up and brought his seemingly lifeless body over to the couch. Once there, Mitch and Foggdog stepped back while I checked out our patient a little further. I was not a qualified doctor but I had been reading a book on emergency care and that pretty much made me the most qualified person in the room.

Art must have come a long way and I was sure there was a reason he was here, but that question would have to wait. I placed my ear near his mouth and looked towards his chest. It wasn't very pronounced, but I could definitely sense it.

"He's breathing," I observed.

"Who is that?" a voice called from up the stairs, accompanied by footsteps. I didn't answer, just continued to monitor Art's breathing trying to make sure he was alive. Mitch and Foggdog couldn't really answer the question, as they didn't know the man's name.

Charlotte made her way down the stairs with Anna in tow, eventually reaching the side of the couch. After taking one look at the man lying there, she placed her hands over her mouth to conceal her shock. She recognized him immediately.

"Is that???" was all she could muster.

"Yes, it's Art," I confirmed. "Can you get us a glass of water, Charlotte? He's breathing; I think he's just exhausted."

Charlotte immediately took Anna into the kitchen, fighting the little girl's desire to get a closer look at what was going on. Foggdog sat back down in his chair, unsure what to do next. After retrieving his gun from the floor, Mitch excused himself.

"I'm going to go back and keep watch, just in case someone was following him," he said.

"Good idea," I agreed. "I don't know that you can do anything here anyway. I think we just need to let him rest and hopefully he'll wake up on his own."

The scene was chaotic. After months of living on our own, including the last few without power, we had unknowingly settled into a routine that was now broken. For as much as I felt prepared for the challenges that we faced, it was always the unknown challenges that seemed to pop up that made me realize how unprepared we really were.

Charlotte re-entered the room with a glass of water and a stack of towels. She placed the water on the coffee table and handed me a towel.

"Thank you," I said. Art was dressed in a navy blue sweatshirt that was completely soaked through from the rain. Underneath, he wore a light gray jumpsuit, which was also soaked through, as were his sneakers. His hair was thinner, grayer, and longer than I remembered (and also sopping wet). His beard was completely foreign – I had never seen him wear one before. We tried to dry him off, but it just didn't seem to be doing any good. His body involuntarily shivered at our touch.

Charlotte rose to her feet and headed away, grabbing a flashlight as she left. We rarely used the flashlights in fear of using their batteries and then not having them when we really needed them.

"Where are you going?" I asked in a tone that suggested I was somewhat annoyed that she was going to use some of the flashlight's precious power.

"This is clearly not working," she replied. "I'm going upstairs to get him some dry clothes and another blanket." She was right, of course, and I watched her as she ascended the stairs with a purposeful grace.

You never quite know the value of your partner until you undergo extreme duress together. When things started getting a little crazy, Charlotte was all-in just like the rest of us. She had as much say in our decision-making process as everyone else and she never wavered in her support of our family. When everyone's focus turned towards our personal survival, it was Charlotte who used her time to focus on Anna's education. While the men grabbed the survival books out of the library and studied up on things like emergency care, farming, hunting, and trapping, Charlotte grabbed the home-schooling guides.

Once she was on a mission, there was no stopping her. It was a challenge to teach Anna one-on-one every single day. She had always been a good student and was very respectful of her teachers. But she often rebelled against her parents, as any child does, and it took a great deal of patience on Charlotte's part before Anna began showing her the same respect she did her teachers.

When I said, "I do," all those years ago, it was under very different circumstances. The possibility of reality turning the way it did was inconceivable. A lesser woman might have given up, but Charlotte is not a lesser woman. Even now, her quick resolve was an asset – the way she scooped up Anna and headed upstairs when an unknown trespasser approached the house or the way she immediately prioritized getting our patient dry as I continued to question whether he was alive.

In no time she was heading back down the stairs, a set of fresh, dry clothes in her arms. She placed the flashlight back down and knelt next to me again and began untying Art's shoes.

"Maybe I should do this instead," I commented, figuring the last thing Charlotte wanted to see was an old, naked man stretched out on her couch.

"Are you jealous?" she asked.

Despite the situation, I chuckled.

"Besides," she continued. "He's been outside in the cold rain for who knows how long. I'm sure he's not going to be in very *impressive* condition."

Did I forget to mention she was also very funny?

We sent Anna out of the room for a few moments as the two of us went to work respectfully stripping Art down, drying him off and dressing him in new, warm, clothes. I checked his breathing again and it still seemed okay. There was really nothing left to do but to keep him dry and warm and hope he would eventually wake up.

By now, Foggdog had resumed his position in the chair and was out like a light. Nothing ever got in the way of Foggdog and sleep when he required it, which was generally more often than the rest of us.

"I guess we should just get some rest," Charlotte said.

"Good idea."

With her usual spot on the couch now occupied by our new visitor, Anna crawled onto the mattress with her mother in front of the fire, taking the position that was usually mine. I re-lit the candles at the far side of the room, but knew there was no way I was going to be able to get to sleep. In a couple of hours it would be my turn to stand watch anyway. Sometimes taking my post with no sleep was better than taking it with too little.

Ascending the stairs, I decided to join Mitch in the lookout perch. It was basically a bedroom we kept dark where one of us sat holding the gun, keeping an eye out for approaching intruders. Since the beginning, we always posted a night watch. As the days and weeks went by, our possessions grew more and more valuable not only to us, but to those around us. We always feared that someone in desperation might just want to go see what exactly was inside the house on top of the hill – one of the few remaining in Liberty Gulch with actual inhabitants. The one time it had happened before made us realize how valuable the simplest items had become – food, batteries, candles, flashlights, toilet paper. We worked hard to obtain and conserve these items and if they were suddenly taken from us, we would be in a world of trouble.

"Is that the same guy…" Mitch started in a low, hushed voice.

"….from the gas station?" I finished, as I sat down in a chair beside him. "Yes. It is."

"Now, correct me if I'm wrong," Mitch continued, "but didn't he used to look a lot different?"

"Yes. Yes, he did." I shifted my weight in the chair, leaning back and glancing towards the sky, not sure what to make of the situation. "His name is Art Brady. I used to know him pretty well – he's a great guy, though he used to be a little more jovial than he looks right now. I wonder what made him come up here?"

"The food."

"Maybe. He would certainly be welcomed here and he would have known that."

"Did he go to the camps?"

"I'm not sure. I haven't seen him since they opened, so maybe he went and then came back. Or maybe he was trying to rough it on his own and finally decided that he needed to reach out for help."

"Well, let's hope he wakes up so we can find out."

We sat in the darkness, peering out of the window. Fittingly, the rain had stopped and the view was getting clearer. The street lights hadn't worked in months, but the moon was full and now that the rain clouds had given way, it lit up the outdoors so you could see the road glistening. There was still a foggy mist hanging in the air. It was indeed a strange night.

After some silent moments, I decided to get back downstairs. "I'd better get back down in case our patient wakes up."

"Good idea. You want to sleep a little longer tonight?"

It was a nice offer, but I had never missed a shift yet and didn't think this was a good enough excuse to start now. "No, it's ok. I'm going to stay up and read a little."

"What's the topic of the evening?"

"I guess I should look up…" I responded, rolling my eyes and thinking of the word.

"The failures of American public schooling?" Mitch quipped as I left the room to head back downstairs.

It was a long running topic of conversation for us. All those years we spent in public school and at college never learning the basics of survival. How do you grow or kill your own food? How do you fix a car? How do you start a fire or fix a bicycle tire? Fixing cars wasn't the type of thing you needed to know if you had a corporate job. But I would have given up all of the finance classes I had ever taken, if I could only know what a carburetor was, or how to shoot a gun, or how to properly clean a fresh kill.

We took those things for granted. They were always done by someone else and never appreciated as much as they should have been. 'Other people' performed practical tasks, which were a commodity in a flourishing economy. But those skills were now invaluable and nobody in the house was particularly handy or knowledgeable about such things.

So we did the only thing we knew how. We hit the books.

The library was one of the only buildings left untouched by the looters. We grabbed as many books as we could and if there was ever any down time, Mitch, Charlotte and I would devour whatever information we needed.

"I think maybe 'how to treat hypothermia' would be a good place to start," I noted before leaving the room.

Heading downstairs, I grabbed a few lit candles off the mantle. Everyone was sleeping soundly except Charlotte, who placed her finger to her mouth and gave me the universal signal to be quiet so that I wouldn't wake Anna. I tip-toed into the office where I grabbed a book off the shelf and sat at the desk to try to figure out how best to treat our sick guest.

The light flickered off the walls and I had trouble focusing given the excitement of the evening. The subject material wasn't exactly gripping, but it needed to be learned. So I dug in and tried to find bits of information we could use to make sure Art was back up and running as quickly as possible. But as I sat there reading in the quiet of night I did something I had never done before. Without setting my alarm to make sure I didn't miss my shift at guard duty, I fell asleep.

CHAPTER TWO

I wasn't sure what woke me from my slumber at first. Picking my head up from the desk, I looked down at the book, whose exposed pages now had a small drool stain on them. As I got my bearings, I realized what had happened and immediately looked down at my watch. "Shit, I'm an hour late for my shift."

Rising from the chair, I heard an unfamiliar cough coming from the living room. It startled me, as for a moment I had forgotten that Art Brady had paid us a visit. Mitch came barreling down the stairs after hearing the coughing man himself, and we narrowly missed crashing into each other.

I pointed at my watch and was about to apologize, but Mitch quickly waved off any such offer. There was a more pressing issue: it appeared our guest was waking up.

As we entered the living room, the coughing became more frequent and pronounced. It was also joined by the sharp scream of an eight-year old, completely freaked out at the strange man who had awoken her. Charlotte tried to talk her down, eventually helping her up from the mattress and bringing her into the kitchen. Perhaps it wasn't a very smart idea to keep Anna in the same room as Art, but it was the warmest place in the house and we weren't going to make anyone bundle up and sleep in a bedroom – especially not a sickly old man or a child.

"Could it get any louder in here?" Foggdog complained, still half-asleep in his chair. I never could figure out how he slept in that chair. It looked impossibly uncomfortable.

As I reached Art's bedside, his body began lurching upward with each new cough.

"Can we take it easy with the coughing, dude?" Foggdog complained further.

I had no patience for this and decided to break the "everybody sleeps downstairs" rule. "Foggdog, get your ass upstairs if you want to sleep. Can't you see this man is ill, you idiot?"

Foggdog grumbled, curled his pillow around his ears and rolled over. I briefly contemplated assigning him to guard duty while Mitch and I checked on Art's well-being, but realized the hypocrisy of such a request after I, myself, had just overslept my assigned watch.

Kneeling at the side of the couch next to Art, I had trouble deciding how best to help him. I wished I had read some of that book. His coughing continued and his hand moved to cover his mouth, which I took as a good sign.

"Can you throw me a towel?" I asked Mitch, who was standing nearest to the stack Charlotte had brought in earlier.

"Sure thing," he replied and tossed it over.

Art's coughing and lurching continued for some moments, and then the old man finally opened his eyes. I could tell he was a little disoriented and unsure of his surroundings, so I tried to comfort him.

"Art, it's okay. You're doing fine, Art. You're safe. It's me Art; it's Ray. Ray Stanton. You walked to my house in the rain. You're going to be fine."

His eyes focused a little better and I could tell that he was beginning to recognize me. The coughing subsided, but was not completely gone. He shuffled himself back up into a seated position. Charlotte returned to the room carrying Anna, who was quick to head back to her spot on the mattress and appeared to fall right back to sleep. Charlotte replaced the old, warm glass of water we had left on the table with a fresh one.

I took the towel from Mitch and cleaned up Art's hands, chin and shirt.

"Thank you," were Art's first words, predictably low and gruff. "I can't believe I made it here. I never thought I'd make it here." He coughed a few more times.

"Well, relax," I said. "You're safe here. You're going to be fine. We're going to nurse you back to health."

Art laughed through the phlegm in his throat, again placing his clenched fist over his mouth. I quickly looked over at Anna, who didn't stir at all. The poor girl was completely exhausted.

Charlotte and Mitch joined me at Art's side as he slowly gained more of his wits about him. He sat up a little further, and began to speak. His voice remained low and gruff, completely estranged from the jovial tone I had remembered fondly.

"There's a reason I came here," he said. "I… I need to tell you."

Mitch and I were immediately captivated and couldn't wait to hear what Art had to say, but Charlotte seemed to know better. "No, Art," she said. "It can wait until morning. You need your rest."

We knew she was right and we couldn't bring ourselves to protest. But we didn't have to, because Art did it for us.

"No," he grumbled. "I need to tell you now. I came all this way and I need to tell you now."

Charlotte's request was quickly pushed aside.

"All this way?" I asked. "Exactly where did you come from, Art?"

"From the food camps, of course!" he rifled back, as if it were a stupid question. "The food camps down at the old Maly Farms, seventeen miles from here." We all knew the camps were at Maly Farms. It had been advertised well enough when they opened. But it was a little more difficult to believe that this old man before us had walked all that way to get here.

"What?" Art protested in his gruff voice. "Oh, you don't think I can make it seventeen miles in the cold rain?"

None of us said a word.

"Well I did, God Dammit. And I made it here, didn't I?"

"Ok, Art. We believe you. Of course, we believe you. And you're welcome to stay here as long as you like."

"I didn't come here for your food," Art shot back. "Or your charity. I came here because I needed to tell someone the truth. I needed to tell someone what is going on at the food camps. It's nothing like what they said it would be; it's nothing like that at all. The people need help. They're dying."

We all crooked our heads in confusion. Maybe this old man had just lost his mind.

"What do you mean, dying?" I asked, concerned that Art might just be a little delusional after coming such a long way.

"Maybe we should resume this conversation in the morning," Charlotte suggested, probably surmising the same thing.

"No," Art insisted, before starting into one of his coughing fits again. We patiently waited for him to finish, gave him a drink of water and then sat back for a minute. The silence was deafening. We wanted desperately to hear what Art had to say, but he was in such poor condition that we didn't know whether or not we could rely on his information. We probably should have let him sleep, but he was fairly insistent that he tell his story.

"All right, look," I started. "Let's just do this. Art, why don't you just start telling your story and we'll keep quiet and listen to what you have to say? If at any point you feel tired, we'll stop."

Art, Charlotte and Mitch all nodded in agreement.

"Let's just start from the beginning, Art. Just tell us everything you remember."

"Ok. Ok. Let's do that." Art reached for his glass of water and took a long, drawn out gulp.

"The bus arrived at Maly and we all filed into line. We were only allowed one bag each, but some people brought more. If you brought more than one, you had to decide which one you wanted to keep and which one you wanted to leave. They took all the extra bags folks brought.

"Then they went through everyone's things. Anything that was deemed a possible weapon was taken. Some people had knives or razors. Even corkscrews were taken. They had told us not to bring guns, but some people still did. They were all taken. Of course the guns were taken.

"We were divided up and assigned our housing. Families with children were likely to be given a trailer. There were hundreds of them lined up in rows. If you weren't assigned to a trailer, you were assigned to a tent. The tents were pretty large, and about as comfortable as you can get for a tent. Three or four people were assigned to each. There were three people in mine, me included.

"Things went pretty well for a while. They fed us and we weren't asked to do much. We could come and go as we pleased. Those that lived close by would often go home for the day and come back for their meals.

"New people kept showing up all the time, so much so that they eventually ran out of tents. So, they grabbed the strongest men and had them build barracks for the newcomers. They weren't fancy – just long, wooden buildings. People slept where they could – on wooden bed frames or on the floor.

"Even with the overcrowding, we all still ate well. Most of us looked forward to returning home as soon as things got normal again."

Art hesitated for a moment. I couldn't tell if he was feeling ill, just taking a breather, or maybe breaking down from whatever emotional experience he had been through.

"Here," I said, offering him some more of the water, which he gratefully accepted. He gulped the rest of the glass down.

"I'll get some more," Charlotte offered. She grabbed the glass and went to the kitchen, returning quickly with a fresh glass of water. Starting at the beginning gave Art a chance to step back and get to a place where he was more comfortable. This part of the story certainly seemed reliable. Art took another quick sip from the water glass before continuing.

"Where was I?" he asked.

"They built the barracks," I said. "Things were normal…"

"Oh, yeah," Art replied. "Things were normal. They were… but not for long.

"Winter came and people were tied down to the farm. Nobody left the premises anymore. It was just too dangerous to do so. As you know, this winter was an especially bad one. The nights were cold and the days weren't much better. We were still fed, but the food quality was noticeably poorer. Soups mostly. Mostly vegetable soup, but occasionally the soup would have chicken in it, and that was a rare treat. Soup every fucking day. It will drive you crazy.

"Then in January, that big storm came."

We certainly remembered that storm. That was the day the lights went out and never came back. It was unexpected, but we were handling it as best as we could. If anything, we were almost getting used to life without electricity.

"Two feet or so of snow," Art continued. "And things became very harsh. The power in the camp went out for weeks and there was no heat. Most people who lived nearby left the camps to use the fireplaces in their homes. There was no heat in the trailers or the tents. People just bundled up in clothes and blankets as best they could to stay warm.

"So the power did eventually come back on the farms?" I asked.

"Eventually, yes. They fixed the lines and the power came back after a couple of weeks," Art answered.

"It never came back here," I explained.

"Not surprising," Art said. "They're not going to go out of their way to help people who haven't reported to the camps. By going out on your own you've told them you don't need any help. If I were you, I'd do my best to prepare for life without electricity. I don't think it's coming back anytime soon."

That thought had certainly entered my mind, though I hoped eventually the power would come back somehow. It was wishful thinking, perhaps. The candles flickered and the fire, now just a few glowing embers, pulsed a gentle light upon the room.

The longer we sat there in the firelight, the more details I could make out about Art's condition. His face was ashen and much more wrinkled than I remembered. His hair wasn't just greyer in color, but it was much thinner as well. His fingers were bony and looked dirty despite his having walked for hours in the rain.

"Where was I?" Art asked. "I keep losing my place."

"The snow storm," I gently reminded him.

"Right," he said and then continued. "Able-bodied men were sent into the woods to collect firewood and we built bonfires for warmth, but it was still very uncomfortable. We struggled through the winter. It seemed as though food kept getting scarcer and, on occasion, someone wouldn't wake up the next morning. And I'm not talking only old men and women. I'm talking children."

Charlotte audibly gasped at the thought of children freezing to death in the camps. It gave Art a chance to collect himself and grab another sip of water. I exchanged eye contact with Mitch. We had always assumed the camps were more comfortable than the house because of all the news reports we had seen before losing power.

Art paused a moment at Charlotte's interruption, but stubbornly shrugged it off and kept on going. "It was at this point that we could sense a change in the government workers. At first, they had been merely organizers – they told us where to go to get food, to get a shower, or go to the bathroom. But slowly they became less and less friendly, and more and more like guards than helpers. After a few incidents of people arguing with them over the food or other privileges, they began carrying guns.

"Over those days people were coming in and out of the camps again, but we could tell something else was going on. The organizers began to use more and more people as laborers. Initially, it seemed we were just helping out – cutting down trees, building barracks, shoveling snow. But over time they expected more from everyone.

"Eventually, those who did the work held contempt for those who left the camps every day for the comfort of their own homes. Why should they work hard for the benefit of everyone else while others got to go home?

"So, one day they passed a rule and people weren't allowed to go home any longer. If you took food from the farm, you had to stay on the farm and you had to work on the farm. People could no longer come and go as they pleased.

"Finally, the weather began to warm up a bit and the snow melted from the fields. We all thought that once the fields began to be prepped for the next year's planting that things would begin to look up. There was one problem though. The tractors all ran on gas, and gas was no longer available. None of us knew why – we weren't told. Did the oil in the Earth finally run out? Could we no longer import it from the Middle East? Were we using all of our oil in our war efforts or was it going to the wealthy? We didn't know – we just knew we didn't have any.

"There was one thing we were all about to learn, though – we were all about to learn how to plow the fields by hand."

Art was getting a little worked up and began coughing again. Once more we handed over the glass of water and he drank while we got a chance to contemplate what we were being told. A clearer picture of what exactly was happening down at Maly Farms was developing, and it wasn't pretty. What was supposed to be a temporary refuge for the hungry and desperate had seemingly turned into a treacherous and deadly labor camp. But one question remained:

"So, Art," I asked as he continued to cough. He truly looked weak and I could tell we were probably doing him more harm than good by keeping him up this late. I tried to push the story a little. "If they needed all those hands in the fields and weren't letting people leave, how did you get here?"

Art settled back into his position, resting his head on the couch pillow before beginning again. He cleared his throat one more time, and continued.

"Escaping wasn't as hard as I thought it would be. There aren't many guards at the camp, and none of them are trained at being guards. They are mostly government employees who were supposed to organize the camp, but the job sort-of morphed into something more. The danger of trying to escape was that they would just shoot first and ask questions later, so nobody ever tried. It just wasn't worth it.

"But after a few weeks working long days in the fields, we began to realize that coming to the camp was the worst decision we ever made. Under the guise of helping us and feeding us, they turned us into slaves and many were extremely upset about it.

"For the most part, there was nothing we could do about our situation. Some people wanted to fight their way out, but the risk was always too great. Most people had families and they just didn't want to risk it. We were all unarmed and there was just no way to overpower the guards, who have shotguns, rifles, pistols – nothing military grade, but enough to keep us in line.

"So, last week we put together a plan."

Art patted at his own chest before looking down and realizing that he wasn't wearing his own clothes any longer. Making this observation, he turned to Charlotte, "Can you please get my sweatshirt for me?"

"Of course," she responded before rising and leaving the room.

"We made a list," he said. "There's a list in the pocket of my shirt."

"A list of what?" I asked.

"It's… you'll see. You'll just have to see."

Charlotte returned with Art's shirt, still soaking wet from the rain. Art took it and reached into the front pocket, producing a stack of white index cards, also soaking wet.

"Damn," Art said. "I tried to keep them as dry as I could."

Art seemed a little frantic and I could see some of the cards ripping in his hands. I didn't know what was on those cards, but apparently it was the primary reason he journeyed here.

"Art, let me take those," I said.

"Hold on," he said, continuing to fidget with them. I dared not reach out to grab them in fear they might tear completely.

"Art. Please give them to me. I will dry them out in the office and then we'll see if we can figure out what's on there."

Looking at the big stack of wet, ripped paper, Art finally gave up trying to piece it all together and surrendered the stack. All I could see in the faint light of the fireplace was blue ink-splotches and some faint letters – many of whose ink had faded or run. I didn't want to disappoint Art, so I got up and brought the cards into the office right away. Placing the whole stack on the desk, I quickly turned around and returned.

I sat back down and Art explained.

"Those cards," he said. "They have information on them."

"What kind of information?" I asked.

"You have to understand," Art said, his voice now nothing but a raspy whisper as he had used up so much of his energy telling his story. "These people are desperate and they need someone to help them. Those cards… they contain the addresses of the people in the labor camp."

I noticed that Art himself had changed his description of the camp from "food camp" to "labor camp." I briefly wondered how many people would have shown up at the "food camps" had they initially referred to them as "labor camps" instead.

"In addition to the addresses, they include anything you need to gain access to those houses – hidden keys, unlocked windows, garage door codes, instructions on how to disarm alarms.

All of these houses have one other thing in common," Art added. "They all have weapons stored somewhere inside – most of them legal, I'm told, but you'll find some rather interesting items on this list. The hope was that I could get this list to someone who would then find and amass these weapons and arrange an assault on the camp."

"Are you kidding?" Foggdog barked from his chair, apparently not sleeping as soundly as we thought.

"I wish I was," Art snapped. "Look, there are people who need help. They will not survive this madness, and they are helpless to fight back. This plan is their only hope."

I turned to make eye contact with Mitch, then Charlotte. Both displayed looks of dismay and doubt. This seemed way too much to ask from a family man just trying to survive on his own.

Art could sense our trepidation. "It doesn't have to be only you. We can amass a force, as many people as we can find. In fact, that's the reason I came here. You're the most natural leader we could think of – smart, prepared, and able to talk sense into people and get them on board. There are plenty of weapons," Art explained, "and the forces arrayed against us are not that strong. They have rifles and pistols only and they're so focused on keeping us in, they will never expect a threat from the outside.

"As long as we plan this quickly, I know the general schedules of the guards including their shift changes in the watchtower. We can hijack a supply vehicle and take them out. We can..." In his excitement, Art began yet another coughing fit.

Charlotte handed him the glass of water, but it didn't seem to do much good. Art's hacking coughs agitated Foggdog once more to the point where he opened his mouth.

"Can't you do something to shut him up?"

"Are you kidding me?" I yelled at him. My patience for my old high school friend had begun to wane over the past few months and I was now pretty much at my wits' end. Had he spoken up again, I might have lost it. I think somehow he understood, because he slinked his way back under his blanket, despite Art's continued outburst.

"Maybe Foggdog is right," Charlotte offered.

"What are you talking about?" I asked, aggravated that my wife was in agreement with the slouch in the chair.

"I think he's had enough for tonight."

Charlotte moved over towards Art's side, taking back the glass of water from his hand. She was right, of course. Once she explained, we all knew she was right.

"He's come a long way," she said, "and he's told his story. I think we all understand what is at stake here. There's no need to get into details right now. We all need to sleep. Art needs his rest and we need to think about what we've just heard and what we are going to do about it."

There was silence for a few moments as Art ceased coughing, pulled up his blanket and turned over on his side. We all took some time to think about what we had just learned.

"It's my watch," I said to Mitch, who nodded in agreement as we all got up from our seats. Charlotte took her place on the mattress next to Anna, who remained sound asleep throughout this whole ordeal. Mitch headed to his own mattress, while I moved towards Art at the couch-side and took a good look at him.

The man had aged a dozen years in less than one. His eyes were now shut and if he was not already asleep, I knew he would be soon. I gently patted his thin, gray hair and thanked him for risking his life to be here before I headed back upstairs to the lookout perch to stand guard the rest of the night.

I don't know if he heard me and I'll never know if he understood my words, because the next morning when we all woke up, Art Brady did not.

THE BEGINNING

CHAPTER THREE

Once we entered the building, Charlotte and I left our cozy, fun-loving relationship behind in favor of our more rigid, "professional" personas. Husband and wife morphed into colleagues and would later reunite again on the way home. It was the small price we had to pay for working at the same firm, but our salaries were good and the convenience of having a similar commute seemed well worth it.

Though we sometimes went to lunch together, for the most part our jobs separated us for the full day so this arrangement wasn't as difficult as it might seem. But the notion that we had to mask our relationship in the company of colleagues sometimes gnawed at me. This was corporate America – no room for private lives. Something about it just didn't feel natural.

Charlotte's office was a few floors below mine and with the elevator otherwise empty we stole a small bit of indiscretion with one last morning kiss before the doors opened and she exited.

Reaching my office, I began my morning routine – which amounted to printing out reports and scanning them for errors or things that didn't belong. It was tedious work, but it kept me busy until our 9am daily meeting, which I always dreaded. In the old days, the meeting would be laid back and enjoyable. But lately they were high-stress and anxiety-filled. We were constantly under pressure to perform better, though I didn't quite fully understand it. The business model was based on a fee structure from our clients. It was a flat fee and as long as our clientele wasn't running for the hills, then our department easily covered its own costs. If anything, we always felt like they should be paying us more.

Five minutes before the meeting, I was called into Mort Randolph's office. Mort was my boss and about twenty years my senior. He was generally a nice guy, but he was one of the biggest sources of the recent stress we were all feeling. Maybe the thought of impending retirement was beginning to get to him; maybe he was undergoing stress at home, or maybe he was just becoming a miserable old curmudgeon. Whatever it was, we just wished he'd get over it.

"Have a seat," he said to me without ever looking up from his desk. I could tell it was one of those rough mornings for him and I was already dreading the 9am meeting enough without having to see a preview.

"Thanks," I replied and took one of the two seats from across his desk.

He shuffled through some papers before swiveling the chair to face me. His eyes seemed exhausted, as if maybe he missed a night of sleep, or perhaps he was even hungover. Knowing Mort for fifteen years, the hangover was my first guess.

"You have always been a great employee and I know you've worked very hard for me," he began. "In a way, I consider you to be like family."

I didn't know where he was going with this, but the mystery behind Mort's red eyes was becoming a bit clearer. There was a small pool of liquid building up in there. It seemed as though he had been... crying. I wondered what the problem was. Was he sick? Was he resigning? I couldn't quite place it, so I had no choice but to wait patiently and listen.

"I know that you have brought a lot of passion to this job and over the years I have been the benefactor of that through the great work we have done together. " He took a moment and sighed, before dropping the bombshell.

"But the decision has been made. We're going to have to let you go."

My shoulders immediately slumped under the weight of the words he had just uttered. Let me go? I was stunned in disbelief and had no idea what to say next, so I just sat there, shocked and confused.

"I want you to know that I fought for you as best I could. They have been asking me to drop headcount for over a year now and I held them off each time. But now this is way over my head."

He waited for me to say something, but there was just silence. The tear welling up in his eye rolled down his cheek. I could see that he was genuinely upset, but I didn't feel like giving into it. There was an anger welling up inside me like none I had ever felt. We had heard rumors of another round of layoffs, but nobody in our group had ever been laid off and there was no reason to think that I would be remotely close to the top of that list.

How could this happen?

This was personal. Regardless of how Mort wanted to frame it, it was personal. One of the problems with the corporate structure was that it extended upwards into echelons where we, not Mort and certainly not I, didn't mingle. And even though Mort might have felt badly about firing me, he was indeed firing me. Maybe I could forgive him one day, but that day was certainly not going to be today. I gritted my teeth before finally breaking the silence.

"Ok… so what next?" I asked, wanting to get this over as quickly as possible.

"There's a representative from Human Resources in the conference room down the hall. They'll have some paperwork for you. Then you'll have an hour to clean up your desk."

"Ok." I got up from my chair.

"Ray," he called. I stood and waited even though he motioned for me to sit back down. Sensing my defiance, he finally spoke. "I know that you may not feel like talking about this now, but when the dust settles, please give me a call. I have some contacts out there and I know some headhunters. We'll get you back on your feet quickly."

I nodded – it was the best I could muster. Head down, I shuffled through the hallway to the conference room, where the H.R. rep filled me in on the rest of the details – severance package, medical coverage, unemployment insurance. It was futile to argue with this man, whose name I now forget. He finished with the paperwork and asked if I had any other questions. I couldn't resist the opportunity.

"Tell me," I started. "Do you get a sense of fulfillment being in this line of work – having to undeservedly fire people you don't even know simply because the masters you work for are too chicken shit to do it themselves?"

He looked at me quizzically, though I'm certain this wasn't the first time he'd been on the receiving end of some vitriolic backtalk from a disgruntled former employee.

"If you're asking if I take pleasure in this part of my job, of course not," he answered. "But Human Resources also does the hiring, and that part of it can, indeed, be very fulfilling."

It felt as though it was a canned response, as if he had read it from a cue card handed out in Firing 101 at Human Resources School. I could only muster one response.

"Fuck off."

It wasn't professional of me, but damn, it felt good and I headed back to my desk with some renewed pep in my step to gather my belongings.

The clock read 9:10 which meant the rest of the department was still in the 9am meeting where they were likely being told that I had been let go and were divvying up my workload. I was glad that they were all away from the desk and I wouldn't have to face them. Though I had an hour until security would come and escort me out, I didn't really need that long. A quick escape seemed like a better idea.

Under my desk was a duffel bag that had been given to me years ago by a salesman. I had thrown it under the desk and never used it or brought it home. It went largely forgotten over the years, but maybe in the back of my head I subconsciously knew I would need it one day. After quickly tossing some stuff in the bag, I hustled my way out of the building for the last time.

On the way out, I couldn't help but think how it was just a few hours earlier that I was walking into the building like I had every day for the past 15 years. Charlotte and I kissed and went to our desks, and then things changed. They changed forever. In the long run I would learn that it was probably one of the best things that could have happened to me.

Now I was in the elevator again, only this time going down hours ahead of schedule. When the doors closed, the weight of the situation began to sink in. How in the world was I going to find a job in such an awful market? How was this going to affect our daily routine? Would we be able to continue to afford daycare for Anna? Even more pressing… how was I going to break the news to Charlotte?

That would have to wait for a bit. I hadn't come to terms with it myself and I thought it best to try to get my own head on straight before hitting her with the bad news. So I walked.

There was nowhere in particular I wanted to go; I just went. Whenever I got to a corner, I looked left and looked right, then walked in the direction that looked most interesting.

Among the bustle of the big city, I found myself in a strange situation. Those around me were all in a rush to get someplace and for the first time I could ever recall, I was not. There was nowhere for me to go, so I slowed my pace. People passed by shooting looks of displeasure at my walking speed.

"To hell with them," I thought.

They all had places to go, but did not see that fact as a gift. For the moment, I envied them. What was I going to do with myself?

That feeling lasted a very short time as I continued to walk with no destination and all the time in the world. After a few blocks I began to relish my slow tempo and even the angst it caused others. Because when I took a step back and thought about it, there was something about this life that I didn't quite understand. Beyond the hustle and bustle, there had to be more meaning.

I came to a park, which had benches lined up along the sidewalk. Taking a seat, I pondered the situation. I thought of Anna and her future. While she grows up in a public school, it had been my plan to spend all of my time working in an office. Something just felt wrong about it. She was my daughter, my responsibility, and I was going to spend most of my waking hours away from her, relinquishing her care to someone else. Maybe there was a better way.

My thoughts raced between confusion, anger, stress, and concern for the future of my family, which up until a few minutes ago was somewhat carefully planned out. I felt very uncomfortable and decided to just sit and watch the people walk by.

The more I watched, the more my imagination began to take over. Instead of people, they seemed more like a herd of wildebeests stampeding along the savannah, not one of them more special than the next. All of them followed the one in front with no vision of the big picture of where they were ultimately headed. Up until today, I had been a member of that herd. It now seemed such an unattractive place to be.

I felt an overwhelming desire to implement some drastic changes to make life more fulfilling and worthwhile. I was convinced that I hadn't been truly living during the course of my working years – I had been just another wildebeest.

As the minutes went by, I became entranced by the stampede. I could hear their footsteps and in my mind their individual figures seemed more like passing shadows. I probably would have sat there for hours had not the buzzing of my cell phone interrupted my daydream.

Fishing the phone out of my pocket, I read the screen: Charlotte.

"Oh, my God, she knows," I thought. The guilt of not telling her what had happened hit suddenly, but I didn't want to worry her.

"Hey, babe," I answered as calmly as I could muster.

"You're not at your desk?" she asked. It felt strange that she didn't say "hello," and went right into a question. But her question suggested that she hadn't found out what happened. She didn't know, which seemed to be a good thing for now.

"No, sorry. What's going on?"

"Can you meet me downstairs?" she asked.

"I can be there in a few minutes. Why? What's going on?"

"You're never going to believe this," she said, her voice cracking just a little bit at the end as if she were hiding emotion. "I just got fired."

CHAPTER FOUR

We picked Anna up from daycare a bit on the early side. She ran around the backyard carrying a football as I watered my vegetable garden, which was coming in nicely. For some reason, she always liked playing with the football – probably because her father watched a lot of it on TV. I couldn't help but teach her how to tackle and how to recover a fumble, which she typically did with great enthusiasm. She still wasn't old enough to catch the ball with any regularity, but she would run with it all over the yard as if she were breaking a kick-off return to win the Super Bowl.

No matter my mood or situation, watching Anna run and play could always make me smile. You would think that after the day we had, I would be a mess trying to sort through it all. But after my post-firing stroll through the city, I was pretty convinced that this was a blessing in disguise. Charlotte's firing... now *that* was unexpected. But I had seen the light and knew that our lives needed to change. Now the trick was convincing my wife.

This was the first year I had ever planted a garden and working on it always gave me a pleasant and tranquil feeling. It was a means of escaping the moment. As I stood there contemplating my strategy for winning Charlotte over, I lost myself somewhat.

"I think they've had enough to drink," Charlotte observed as she walked onto the porch of our rented home. She was right, indeed they had. The water was beginning to pool in spots and with my mind wandering, I just hadn't noticed.

"Why don't you put the hose away and come inside? The pizza is here and after we finish eating, we'll get Anna off to bed a little early so we can discuss this."

I remember her calmness amidst a perceived moment of turmoil. She was graceful and unflinching. She kept herself together and, if anything, seemed confident that everything would be okay.

We ate our pizza and made light-hearted conversation with Anna about her day at daycare. When we finished, I wrapped the leftover slices in foil and put them in the fridge. I always had trouble throwing away food, despite knowing I would never eat the pizza I was wrapping.

Charlotte gave Anna a bath and then I helped her to bed. We read a few books together, though I largely glossed over the words without much thought. Anna stopped me a number of times because she could tell my tone was somewhat different than normal. She was just like her mother – smart as a whip. Nothing ever got by her. I plowed my way through the books and kissed her good night before turning out the light.

"Good night, Anna," I whispered, trying to seem as calm as I could, which was as much for my own benefit as it was for hers.

"Good night, Daddy."

Returning to the living room, I found Charlotte on the couch in front of the television with two mojitos mixed and poured into tall glasses. Mojitos are not my kind of drink – certainly not something I would ever order in a restaurant or bar. But we had mint growing in the garden and Charlotte knew how much I liked to use any of the ingredients from there. It was a personal victory each time something tasty came out of that garden.

We sat and talked about the day we had both had – how our firings went down and how our bosses, who we once considered teammates, if not confidants and mentors, handled the stresses of letting us go. We made ourselves laugh not because it was funny, but because we didn't know how else to deal with the obvious.

We were avoiding the topic, but eventually we could no longer ignore it: What the hell were we going to do now?

I spoke openly about my experience at the park and how, in a way, today's events were somewhat liberating. Going to work for all those years had worn me down. It wasn't fun, it wasn't enlightening, and over time the need for a paycheck was the driving force behind showing up every day. I wasn't proud of myself or how I spent the bulk of my time. I worked because I had to; because my parents had instilled in me the value of a secure job with good benefits. I had worked so hard to achieve it, and now it was all gone.

What was the purpose of it all?

Though it had paid quite well, our work was not personally fulfilling to either of us. The sedentary lifestyle of daily office life was unhealthy. We were confined to touting the party line and never felt free to have an opinion outside the realm of popular thought. We were at the constant whim of our bosses, who could keep us in the office late at night or make us come in on weekends. Through our jobs, we had become mindless creatures of habit. We were more like servants, wittingly subjecting ourselves to tasks for which we had no particular interest or love because we felt as though we had no other choice.

Surveying our options, the divergence in our opinions couldn't have been wider. I was trying to find a silver lining of opportunity that might lead us away from re-entering the dreary world to which we had become accustomed. Charlotte seemed to be handling the situation much more sensibly.

"We get up tomorrow, put our resumes together and start pounding the pavement. We have a daughter to raise and we can't fuck around."

She could be so eloquent sometimes. I could tell that her initial inclination to stay in the business world was not going to be something she would easily rethink. Over the course of the next few hours I would try my best to chisel away at it, so that we could at least survey all of our options.

But after hours of gentle prodding and light cajoling, it seemed as though we were headed to bed undecided. I was confident in my own mind, but I was quite sure that Charlotte thought I was a little crazy. I put forth a final proposition. "Instead of looking at our situation as an obstacle to be overcome, what if we looked at it as an opportunity we will likely never have again?"

We each had 10-months worth of severance pay ahead of us and unemployment insurance would pay on top of that. We didn't have much in the way of financial commitments – no debt in the form of student loans, credit cards or a mortgage. In fact, we had built up a good deal of savings over the years. Of course, this was mostly to be used as a down payment on our dream home in the suburbs and to fund a comfortable retirement after sending Anna to college, but now I was having second thoughts.

"Look, all I'm saying is that we've given our lives to this business and look what happened. Maybe we just need to take a step back and figure out what we *want* to do instead of what we *have* to do. Let's not put the resumes together just yet. Let's give it a week to soak in and see how we feel after that."

She didn't say anything, but I could swear that I saw Charlotte give the slightest nod. It was starting to get late, and the thought that she might just be placating me for the time being crossed my mind. Regardless, it felt like a step in the right direction. Gathering the empty glasses from the coffee table, I got up from the couch.

I flicked off the television and reached to turn off the light. In the momentary silence we were suddenly startled by the sound of glass shattering and a metal object rolling across the hardwood floor. We both jumped back, and then looked at each other. A brief lull of confusion followed before the flash-bang grenade exploded.

The noise was deafening and the accompanying flash made it feel as though a bomb had exploded in our living room! Surely we were dead.

Charlotte jumped in my arms, though I wasn't sure that I could offer her much comfort because I was in just as much shock. The front door was forced open from the outside and multiple armed men in black body armor carrying automatic weapons filed into our home, yelling "Police!"

My first instinct was to raise my hands in surrender. I had no weapon, no defense. Charlotte followed my lead and did the same.

As guests in our home, the men were not very cordial. They grabbed our arms and roughly threw us face down on the floor. Temporary cuffs were placed on our hands and we both felt the pressure of a knee weighing heavily on our backs. I couldn't understand why these men were here in our home.

As we lay there stunned, the saddest sound slowly became audible. It was Anna from her upstairs bedroom, screaming uncontrollably. The volume of the screams grew somewhat when I noticed one of the men descending the stairs with our innocent little daughter in his arms.

There was nothing I could do. I had never felt so helpless. The knee in my back and the gun barrel at the base of my head was proof of that. Placing my head down on the floor, I closed my eyes and could only listen as Anna cried out for her Mom and Dad. They were certainly not going to obey her screaming requests. I could do nothing but wait for an explanation as to why this was happening. The smell of the grenade still hung in the air. I'll never forget that smell. It was the smell of a defeated man – just fired from his job and now helpless to protect his own family.

Anna always slept so soundly and I wondered what had awakened her – was it the glass shattering, the grenade blast or the officers storming in? How frightened she must have been when men dressed in black suits carrying weapons kicked open her door.

My helplessness quickly changed into fury. We were not criminals. We were law-abiding citizens. My initial reaction was to just do as we were told. The police are there to protect us, so they must have had a reason to be here. I accepted that… until I saw Anna. What kind of devastation had they just done to the psyche of our little girl, who was now probably in some social worker's car being told that "everything will be all right."? I could not think of anything more traumatic for a child to experience and I was powerless to help her.

How would I ever again be able to tell her, "Don't worry, daddy will protect you," and provide her with any true feeling of security?

We were brought to the police station, booked, and kept in separate holding cells. Our lawyer appeared about an hour later and spoke to both of us individually. It didn't take them long to realize that, indeed, a mistake had been made.

We had rented that house and had been living in it for just over three months. Before that time, the resident was some sort of blogger who had recently leaked confidential material on the internet. Whatever it was, it must have been pretty serious stuff, because instead of just going to the door and knocking, the police set up a quick sting at his last-known address. Expecting to find a solitary man behind a laptop, they must have been confused to see us there. Of course, we were a little more surprised to see them.

After being emotionally reunited with Anna, who was still in tears, the police apologized – which was the most we were ever going to get out of them, at least until the settlement. Our lawyer drove us home. He was a nice guy, and when the bill came a few weeks later, I understood why. While I cannot say that he didn't earn his pay that evening, it hurt to write that check knowing I was only doing so because some asshole cops made a mistake. Months later, the settlement eased that pain a little, but there is no cost worth the damage that night might have done to our daughter.

We got home in the early morning hours under the cover of darkness. Anna had never slept a night in our bed before. We wouldn't allow it. But things seemed different this time. As the sun began to rise, the three of us climbed under the blanket together.

Just 24 hours earlier, our alarms had rung signifying the start of just another ordinary day. Oh, how things had changed.

"I think it's safe to say," Charlotte observed, "this has been the worst day of our lives."

I agreed. It seemed a pretty safe assumption at that time.

"Ray?" Charlotte added.

"Yeah, babe."

"I think I'm ready to make a big change."

"Okay."

CHAPTER FIVE

Our list of priorities for our new home was relatively small. I wanted good land at a good price. Charlotte insisted there be a good public school system for Anna. We both wanted a house that comfortably fit our family while having good storage space and room for guests if we could ever talk our friends and family into coming to visit us out in the middle of nowhere. Above all, we wanted to be as financially secure as possible and not have to rely on anyone.

Even before the settlement with the police department, we had been saving money for years to buy a home in the suburbs. Real estate was outlandishly expensive in the areas around the city, but this was where we wanted to live before this whole episode began. The schools were all top-notch and it was an easy train ride into the city. An expenditure that size was a major investment, so we rented our last home there just to make sure that we liked the neighborhood beforehand. What a great decision that turned out to be.

Having no house to sell gave us the freedom to just pick up and leave. So, leave we did.

The discount for living in a rural setting away from the traffic of the big city was incredible. For what would have been a good-size down payment on an average house in suburbia, we were able to purchase just as much house on a large swath of land without a mortgage. The home was ours free and clear, and we still had money to spare.

Of course, this took us quite a distance from the city with which we had become so familiar. But in that one day the world had changed so much for us that we were desperate to make a permanent change. We found that new life in a small country town called Liberty Gulch.

The real estate agent drove us along a long road that had a persistent, yet subtle upslope. As the road came to a dead-end, an old oak tree marked the entrance to a driveway – a regal giant that immediately caught our eye as we crested the hill. The tree gave the house behind it some added character and charm, not that it necessarily needed it. Passing by the noble guardian, the house revealed itself. When we first saw it, we knew right away it was the one for us.

It wasn't very old, at least not in house-years and certainly not older than the tree that guarded its entrance. It was a medium-sized, two-story colonial home painted a light yellow. A large front porch wrapped around the left side, with the mandatory porch swing towards the back. You could pull the car right next to the side door of the house, or you could continue on a few feet to the detached garage, which looked like a small barn and was painted to match the house.

Inside, the house was as comfortable as it looked from the outside. The rooms weren't huge, but having lived in city apartments for much of our lives, we were used to smaller spaces. For us, this house had more space than we would ever need.

It had a fairly large front and backyard – one I was not looking forward to mowing. But I was going to have plenty of time on my hands and it turned out to not be as bad as I feared. The backyard was flat with plenty of space for my garden, which would continue to provide me with peace from the real world. The property itself extended multiple acres into the woods behind. There was a lake back there somewhere, but we didn't even care to hike to it before the papers were signed. Neither of us wanted to stay in that rented home any longer than we needed, so we moved into the new place as soon as we possibly could.

We endeared ourselves to our new home and our new life immediately. I knew that Anna would adapt quickly. Little kids always do. We had hardly had time to get used to our rented home in the suburbs and didn't have many planted roots. It was Charlotte that concerned me, but she showed remarkable strength and enthusiasm.

We scraped by that first year and, though it felt good not to have to rely on others for our well-being, we both started feeling a little bored and decided that a little income couldn't hurt. So, both of us took part-time jobs to earn some extra money. It was important to us that we not feel like we had strict schedules to which we had to adhere, or bosses we had to impress. Even with the new jobs, the shackles were still off and we couldn't have felt better about it.

Charlotte worked at a jewelry store in town run by a nice, old fellow named Morris Roberts. For years, Morris ran the store with his wife, but she had sadly passed away shortly before we moved to Liberty Gulch. Charlotte saw Morris putting the "Help Wanted" sign in the window and asked him about it right away. She was no snooty jewelry collector. In fact, other than her engagement ring, she hardly had anything of significant value. But living in the city for years, she often spoke with her co-workers and friends about jewelry and she had, rather accidentally, become somewhat knowledgeable in the trade. That is to say she was more knowledgeable than most Liberty Gulch residents who might seek employment there.

As an employee, Morris loved Charlotte. How could he not? She was smart, worked hard, and never bothered him for a raise or hassled him over working conditions.

I was able to get a part-time position as a loan officer at the Liberty Gulch National Bank under similar circumstances. The bank's CEO took one look at my qualifications and wanted to know why I only wanted part-time employment. I just told him the truth – I wanted to work to stay busy, but I never wanted to feel completely beholden to a job again. I didn't know if that answer was going to fly, but I think he actually appreciated my honesty, and so I was hired.

We fell in love with our quaint new town and after three years we no longer considered ourselves city-folk.

It was a warm night in early June. Charlotte got Anna to bed early and we stayed up reading. In the old days we used to watch TV all night, but the move to the country changed a lot about us. As our environment changed and as Anna grew older, we became much more independent in nature. We were less inclined to engage in meaningless, time-wasting ventures. In the context of how much of our lives' time had been wasted watching mindless TV, it was overwhelming. I never considered it such until I got out here and life became more about living and less about conforming to a set schedule or succumbing to the voyeuristic allure of reality television.

We read books. Lots of books. I read, Charlotte read, but the most voracious reader in the house was certainly Anna.

"We finished <u>Stuart Little</u> tonight," Charlotte reported.

"Already?" I asked. "She just started it yesterday!"

"She spent most of her day reading," Charlotte answered. "It was raining earlier so we were mostly indoors."

"She's really taken to reading. I guess I shouldn't complain," I said rather proudly. "What's next on the docket?" I asked.

"I don't know. We don't have anything in the house she hasn't read. And I have a bit of bad news for you," she said. "The books are due back at the library tomorrow."

"Oh shit," I exclaimed, having completely forgotten about the library books. It was a Friday night and I had hoped it would be another few days before I had to head back down the hill to town.

"It can be a few days late, you know – just pay the late fee," Charlotte suggested, knowing very well that I would never agree to that. Lateness was a pet peeve of mine and I'd be damned if I would set a bad example for Anna.

"I don't think I want the Library Police at my doorstep."

"You remember the last time the police arrived at our doorstep," she reminded me.

I didn't need to answer that. Of course I remembered. Ever since that night we had worked towards repairing Anna's innocence. She often had nightmares, waking up screaming and saying she saw men with guns in the house. We tried not to relive the incident, but we certainly understood why she would think such a thing. No matter how many times I explained to her that no men with guns were ever going to come into the house, part of me always questioned my ability to make such a promise. After all, it had happened once before.

The next morning Anna and I hopped in the truck and headed down the hill to return her books and pick out some new ones. The sky was overcast and the air smelled of impending rain. We were expecting a storm, but not a big enough one to hinder our trip down the hill into town. For as much as Charlotte's suggestion of returning the books late was tempting, I simply could not allow it.

As soon as we got out from under the cover of our oak tree, the pitter-patter of the first drops hitting the windshield began. Anna talked about some of the books that were on her reading list and which ones she wanted to search out at the library. I can't remember being as enthusiastic for reading at that age, though I have vague memories of the library being a lot more fun as a child than as a college student or an adult. I am not sure what dulls a child's lust for knowledge over the years – maybe it's a combination of the rigidity of school curricula or the peer pressure from those less enlightened. But I was determined not to allow these influences to reach Anna any time soon.

As we traveled, the rain got progressively worse. At times I strained to see the road, but only when we reached town did it become almost completely blinding. The pitter-patter had changed to more of a constant deluge of water pouring down on the truck. Anna chatted away in the back seat, but I could barely concentrate as I leaned forward to get my eyes closer to the windshield. We made the turn by Art Brady's gas station where the Liberty Gulch Public Library would normally be in sight, but it was impossible to view on this day.

Being extra cautious, I slowly pulled the truck into the parking lot of the 4-story brick building, the largest in Liberty Gulch. Lightning crackled and thunder rumbled as we opened the doors to make a dash for it. Jumping from the truck, we hustled through the parking lot dodging rain drops, each footstep finding a puddle until we reached the doors. Though we had only gone a short distance, our clothes were soaked through. Looking down at ourselves, there was nothing we could do but laugh.

Anna pulled Stuart Little and a few other books out from under her shirt, where they had remarkably stayed dry, and handed them over to the librarian. Mrs. Quigley was a very sweet lady probably in her 50's or so, with short, curly gray hair and glasses. She was always fond of Anna, who had to be her most frequent 8 year-old client.

But, before she even had a chance to say hello, Anna had already fled towards the stacks. Making eye contact with Mrs. Quigley, I just shrugged. "I guess she can't wait to read the next one," I commented. "Five million books in the library and I think at this pace she might get to all of them."

We shared a smile before I went off to follow my little girl, who was now skipping through the aisles towards her favorite section.

The first few times we had gone to the library, about three years ago, all Anna wanted to do was go in the corner and play with the toys that were scattered about. One of us, either Charlotte or I, would try to keep an eye on her while the other searched for appropriate books. After some time, Anna realized that she wanted to have a say in her bedtime reading material too. So, she would follow us through the rows of books and we would pick some out to show to her for approval.

Of course, by now she was an expert. No longer did we have to pick books out for her and no longer did she have any affinity for the toys in the corner. We just left her alone and she would take her time scanning through the titles, looking at the covers, and eventually finding her next treasure. Today she brought back two books – Charlotte's Web by E.B. White and The Hobbit by J.R.R. Tolkien.

"Two of my favorites," I observed.

"Which one should we read first, Dad?" she asked.

She seemed really young for Tolkien and I briefly wondered if the book was placed in the wrong section. Just looking at the two, I knew there was quite a difference between them. But it would be challenging for her and I wasn't going to stand in her way if she had an interest in a classic novel, even at this age. I knew if she had trouble, Charlotte or I would always help out. Having seen her enjoyment in reading Stuart Little, I figured back-to-back E.B. White novels might not be a bad idea. Besides, she seemed to get a kick out of the fact that this book had her mother's name in it.

"Let's read this one first," I said, pointing to Charlotte's Web.

"Ok, Dad." She took her new books and skipped back through the aisles, her father following in tow.

Mrs. Quigley stamped the books and handed it over to Anna along with a purple lollipop – her favorite.

"Have a nice day, Anna."

"Thank you, Mrs. Quigley."

"You have a nice day too, Mr. Stanton," Mrs. Quigley said to me.

"Back into the rain we go," I remarked.

"Actually," Mrs. Quigley observed, "It looks like the rain has stopped and the sun is coming out."

Sure enough, we looked towards the glass doors where a ray of bright sunshine illuminated the lobby.

"Wow, I guess it is," I acknowledged.

Walking out into the parking lot, the ground was still damp and a few puddles that had formed from the rainstorm were still evident.

"Daddy, can you hold my books?" Anna asked.

"Of course."

I took the books and watched as Anna went and jumped into the puddles. She knew we didn't like her to get all wet and dirty, but she was wearing an old pair of shoes that were starting to get a little too small for her and I just couldn't say, "No."

After that night when the police broke in all those years ago, I could never resist allowing her to enjoy the harmless pleasures that children garner from simple acts like jumping in a puddle. A grown-up would never think of doing such things. Her innocence was an inspiration to me and I took in the scene for what it was – a little girl joyously stomping in a puddle, not caring at all about getting wet or dirty, but just having fun.

"Look, Anna," I pointed out. "Look up there."

Up in the sky, in the wake of the rain and the oncoming sunshine, was a beautiful, full rainbow. It traced the sky from horizon to horizon.

"It's beautiful, daddy," she said, pointing at the sky with a child-like awe.

It was a perfect moment. My beautiful, innocent daughter stood gleefully in a puddle having fun in a raw, natural fashion, untainted by human sin and envy. In my hands, I held the books that marked her advanced reading ability – the key to knowledge, but perhaps also the gateway to adulthood – while above us hung the beauty of nature in the bright, clearing sky. I had seen plenty of rainbows before, but this one was easily the most impressive.

I took out my cell phone and snapped a picture of Anna in the puddle, the prettiest girl in the world with the prettiest rainbow in the sky behind her. The picture was perfect and I immediately made it the wallpaper image on my cell phone, so that I could see it every time I turned it on. In that moment, everything seemed perfect, as if I had finally gotten over worrying about the lasting effects of that awful night.

But the wheels of a bigger problem had been set in motion years ago. In a few minutes I would see the very first sign of what was to come. Had I known this was the last moment of purity I would have for a long time, I might have enjoyed it longer.

"Let's get in the car," I said.
Anna stopped playing in the puddle.
"Ok, Dad."

CHAPTER SIX

We left the parking lot and headed back towards home. The sun shone brightly, beginning the arduous task of evaporating the remnants of the rain. Riding with the windows down, we could smell the moisture in the air as the tires of the truck swished through the leftover puddles in the street.

Two blocks down was Art Brady's gas station. The gas gauge indicated a little under a quarter-tank, so I pulled in to top it off.

The pump at Art's gas station never seemed to work properly. Pernicious smells leaked from the nozzle signifying something wasn't properly sealed. It was probably not a healthy thing to inhale, but I found a certain pleasantry to the fumes.

Everything always seemed to need gas – the lawn mower, the weed-whacker, the snowblower and the generator. I always kept a number of full containers in an area where, if it happened to blow up, nobody would get hurt. When the tanks were emptied, I threw them in the back of the truck and filled them the next time I got to the gas station. Today, I was in the midst of filling three extra containers when I saw the station's proprietor and my friend, Art Brady, make his way from his store over to the price board near the corner.

Art was a man in his early-60's who seemed to know everyone in town. That wasn't surprising, since he ran pretty much the only gas station. Everyone needed to fill-up there and Art was a friendly guy.

He trudged his way through the puddles, his hands holding a stack of numbers. Always the pessimist, I guessed he was about to drop his prices just as soon as I filled my tank. Things always seem to work that way, don't they? I topped off the first can and set it into the bed of my pick-up. Anna sat inside reading one of her new books, and seemed to be sufficiently keeping herself busy. I stood by for a moment, only to watch Art Brady replace the current $3.75/gallon price with a new number... $7.25.

Taking a quick look at the pump, I confirmed the price I initially knew. Yes, it read $3.75.

It must be a joke, I thought. Art always had a good sense of humor and my sense was that this was just some kind of prank he was pulling on someone. Even so, I made sure to top off all my gas containers as much as they would take.

Art walked back towards our direction as I closed the nozzle on the final gas can and went to begin filling the truck.

"Good afternoon, Ray" Art said.

"Hey Art, good to see you," I responded.

Art bent over slightly and gave a wave to Anna inside the truck. She was so deeply in the book already that she didn't even notice. I was tempted to knock on the window to insist she politely say hello, but Art stopped me in mid-motion.

"Don't bother, Ray," he said. "She looks pretty busy and besides, there are worse things kids can be doing than reading a book."

I gave a polite laugh to his keen observation, though I wished Anna was a little more respectful towards her elders.

"Make sure you top it off as much as you can," Art added. "You got here just in time."

"Wait... are you saying that the price up on that sign is real?"

Art gave a big sigh and placed his hands on his hips. "I just got the call from the office. Prices gotta go up, so I put 'em up."

"Did they give you any idea why?" I asked. We had grown accustomed to the near $4/gallon we had been paying, and it had always fluctuated between the three and four dollars the past few years. To jump all the way to seven-and-change seemed very harsh.

"I don't have an explanation," Art admitted. "Speculators, I guess. At least, that's what they told me last time prices jumped."

"Speculators," I nodded in agreement, knowing full well that it was the typical excuse politicians used to blame Wall Street for price increases. But I knew better than to argue with Art over it, and just appreciated his effort at an explanation. "That's probably it."

"I wouldn't worry about it too much," Art added. "This is only a temporary thing. No politician would ever get re-elected with seven dollar gas. They'll do something to fix it. I bet the next time you're down here it'll be back under five bucks."

"Yeah," I said. "You're probably right." I was hoping for a better explanation and the lack of one made me a little bit nervous. I rejected the receipt from the pump before thanking Art one last time for allowing me to fill up at the low price before raising it. Then he retreated back to his office in the convenience store attached to the station.

On occasion, Charlotte would accuse me of being paranoid. Always fearing the worst, sometimes I just felt an inner need to be secure. "Hope for the best, but plan for the worst," my father used to say. It was good advice and had never done me wrong.

My intuition told me that everything was connected to gas prices because all commodities needed to be transported to stores to be sold. If gas prices could double in an instant, what might happen to food prices? And what would happen if gas prices doubled again tomorrow? Maybe I was being paranoid, but I thought about my Dad's advice and decided we had one more errand to run.

"Anna, we're going to make a pit stop at the grocery store before going home. Ok?"

"But I want to go home and show Mom my new books," she whined. "This one has her name in it," she observed, holding the E.B. White novel up high.

I shot her the evil eye. Not the super-evil "you're in trouble" evil-eye but the, "Are you really going to give me shit over this" evil-eye. No words were needed.

"Ok, dad," she capitulated in a gruff, protesting tone.

On a gut feeling, I went back through town to its lone grocery store. We were always pretty stocked up at the house, but I just wanted to make sure we were better supplied in case gas prices didn't come down as Art had predicted and the price of food escalated.

I wheeled the cart around the store and Anna faced me from the other side. Her feet were up on the bar of the far end of the cart and she was having fun going for a ride. She was laughing and enjoying herself, while I focused on finding items with a longer shelf life that we could stock up on. I felt like it was the night before a snowstorm and I was hunkering down by taking everything off the shelves. Only, I was going a little bit overboard.

I grabbed boxes of dried pastas, cases of canned goods and bags of white rice – nothing that would spoil too quickly. The storage freezer in the basement at home was already half-full, so I bought enough meat to fill the other half. I grabbed candles, a couple of extra flashlights and Anna and I just about cleaned out the whole store of batteries. Certainly I was overreacting, but if we woke up tomorrow and gas was twenty bucks a gallon, the whole town would be in a panic and I would never be able to secure these supplies at today's prices.

Anna smiled as we turned the corner of the last aisle with two overloaded carts and headed for the register. When I thought about it, I was just weighing my fear of being seen as "paranoid" against the security of being prepared for the worst case scenario. That thought alone was just the confirmation I needed that I was doing the smart thing. It just seemed better to have too much than too little.

We checked out at the cashier and headed back up the hill towards home. The ride was fairly quiet as the weather had fully cleared and Anna attacked more of her new book. Sitting in the front alone and going up the same hill I had gone up hundreds of times over the past few years, my mind began to wander. We had moved up here because we were tired of the hustle and bustle of the corporate world and we wanted to start something fresh, outside of the realm of what we had always known. We liked rural living and believed we had enough savings to live comfortably for the rest of our lives while only taking on part-time jobs… or so we thought.

If ten-dollar, twenty-dollar, or thirty-dollar gas was part of the next paradigm, would we be able to continue our early semi-retirement? I just didn't know. Looking back, that should have been the least of my worries.

We arrived home and Anna ran into the house with her new book, speeding right by her mother who was working on our laptop computer at the kitchen table. I followed behind with two armfuls of bags and my fresh sense of impending doom.

"Hey, how was the library?" Charlotte asked, with a questioning look after seeing me carrying a whole new bunch of groceries.

"Mom, Mom," Anna said excitedly, running back into the kitchen. "Look what I got! She showed her mother her latest book.

"Wow," Charlotte replied with a smile.

"It has your name in the title, Mom."

"I see that. <u>Charlotte's Web</u>. Now this is a great book."

Anna didn't waste any time with further small talk. She took the book back from her mother and went into the other room, presumably to continue reading where she had left off in the car.

I dropped off the bags in the kitchen and quickly made my way to the living room. Avoiding any further conversation, I reached for the remote control under some magazines and turned on the television set.

Charlotte trailed me into the living room, sensing that something was amiss.

"What's going on?" she asked as the television lit up with news reports of the incredibly quick doubling of gas prices.

"I'm not quite sure," I said. "But I think it's time to find out."

CHAPTER SEVEN

These past few years we tried our best to escape the clutches of mainstream news media and television in general, but world events seemed to lead us there anyway. We believed that not watching television had grown into a healthy habit of sorts – a habit we now found ourselves often breaking.

Charlotte and I decided to take a few days off from our part-time work and stay in the house. We felt it was important to watch the events unfold and stayed true to our pledge not to let our jobs run our lives, even if we were spending these days doing what we never did – watching television.

The price of oil was skyrocketing and with it went gas prices across the nation. Every channel seemed to be covering it – reporters in the commodities pits, on the trading floors, and at the gas pumps. People were in an uproar, with bouts of violence at the pumps video-taped on cellphone cameras being displayed across the internet. There were few legitimate explanations as to why we were seeing the price increase. Tensions in the Middle East were high, but when had they not been?

Three days into the gasoline panic, prices now stood at the scary level of nearly $25/gallon and there was still no apparent catalyst driving the events. As I had rightly predicted, the grocery store shelves were getting thin as shipments were delayed in the hopes that prices would fall.

Charlotte quipped, "I guess it was a good idea to stock up the house for a few years." Her intention was for that to be a joke, but in reality she wasn't exaggerating all that much – I had really stocked up for the long haul that day and if we had to, we could survive on our stores alone for quite some time.

After these three days the public had grown outwardly frightened and there was finally a government response, which brought the familiar charge:

"It's because of the evil speculators."

In a way, Art was right, because the politicians decided they had had enough and went to work applying a number of new measures and regulations – strategic oil reserves were tapped, price controls and rationing of gasoline and some food products were implemented. Regulators were on a heightened lookout for market manipulators, with maximum penalties being threatened should charges be proven.

For a few days this almost seemed to work. Tensions seemed to calm, fears seemed to subside and prices even came down a few bucks on their own. It was still extremely expensive for trucks to transport basic needs like food from the farms to the cities and the prices of all goods were rising accordingly, but the general thinking was that the worst was behind us.

"I think I'm ready to head back to work," Charlotte said. "I'm going to give Morris a call and tell him I'll be in tomorrow."

"Probably a good idea," I admitted cautiously. I wasn't fully convinced that the worst of these events were behind us, but we had been home for over a week and it was admittedly getting a little monotonous sitting around the house most of the day.

As much as I thought we were not necessarily in the clear, I hadn't the conviction in my belief and felt as though it was just another bout of paranoia. Subconsciously, maybe I just wanted to hope for a return to normalcy. But then the television blared with a report of "BREAKING NEWS." There had been a lot of "Breaking News" the past few days and you could always count on the networks to over-sensationalize the smallest developments. But this one seemed a bit more important.

A number of countries including China and Russia had decided to come together and merge their currencies. Unlike all of the major currencies in the market, they would back this one with a basket of real assets such as gold and silver, along with other currencies such as the US Dollar, Euro, British Pound and Yen. The move was unexpected, shrewd, and an immediate game changer for the global economy.

Historically, the purchase and sale of things like oil was always done in the world's reserve currency, the U.S. dollar, but now that was no longer necessary. There was a stronger currency on the block and the oil producers were happily pronouncing their willingness to accept it. Panic ensued almost immediately.

Once again stock markets tanked, interest rates rose, and commodity prices skyrocketed as the value of the dollar itself was now in question.

"They knew," I said.

"What do you mean?" Charlotte asked.

"That's the reason gas prices went up. People knew this was coming and they got ahead of it."

She let my observation hang there for a while and we continued to follow the market developments. My mind raced as I watched, wondering what could possibly happen next. It was all so much to digest and I had this overwhelming feeling that things could only get worse. Perhaps through a bit of luck, I had been ahead of the curve topping off the gas tanks and stocking up on food supplies, but it seemed as though I was still missing something. It was always just a matter of trying to stay one step ahead of what was going to happen next, but I couldn't think of a proper course of action.

A few moments after the initial announcement, there was already buzzing out on the streets. Cameras bounced around to a number of different locations and in-studio reports, before they found a somewhat familiar street location.

The reporter on the street now stood not two blocks from the very building where Charlotte and I had worked just a few years back. As I watched people being interviewed along the crowded streets, I sensed a certain tension or perhaps even fear. People were all in a rush and yet it was the middle of the day. Why weren't they at their desks?

"Is that?" Charlotte asked.

"Yes, just two blocks from work," I replied.

"No," she said. "Look there."

In the background was a branch of our old bank, where we used to hike the extra two blocks to hit the ATM in order to avoid the extra fees they would charge us if we used the machine in our building. The place was buzzing with people and a line had formed far down the block out of view from the camera.

And then it made sense.

With stocks getting crushed and interest rates soaring, people were seeing the writing on the wall. Their concern turned to the reliability of the banks' financial health. They began ditching their desks and getting their ass on line at the bank to get their money out as quickly as possible.

It was the dreaded "bank run."

The line at the bank grew, and eventually it could extend as long as it wanted. But at some point people were not going to be able to get their money. Though the government had set up an insurance program to protect against such an occurrence, this just seemed different. The FDIC was set up to protect investors from smaller bank failures, but when the bigger banks started getting into trouble, full-blown bailouts were necessary.

"There are few iron-clad guarantees in life" began the FDIC propaganda piece now being played on the screen, "but this is one of them."

I was mad at myself for believing the prevailing thought that things were improving. Mad at myself for not trusting my gut. And now my concern, which I had once thought was merely paranoia, was replaced with a new feeling: Fear.

I grabbed my keys.

"Where are you going?" Charlotte asked.

"To get our money."

I jumped into the truck and sped down the hill as fast as I could. Two miles of winding roads seem to take forever when you're in a mad dash. Outside of our retirement accounts, we had most of our savings in that bank and I wanted to get as much of it as I could in my hands as quickly as possible.

After what seemed like way too long, I arrived at the Liberty Gulch National Bank thinking I was already too late. The small parking lot was a little more full than usual and when I walked in, the line was about ten customers deep, which was longer than I'd ever seen in the small country bank. I sensed that many were there for the same reason I was, but nobody was talking about it.

One of the benefits of living in a small town was that people were typically busy caring for their own business and had little time or desire to monitor world events. Unlike the big city, where you couldn't miss it because it was all around you, the residents of Liberty Gulch largely had no idea the bank run had begun.

Even though I was a part-time employee at the bank, I still had to wait in line like everyone else. So, I waited patiently and quietly as the tellers took care of the customers, not knowing if I had made it there in time. I knew how much cash they typically kept in the safe, and it wasn't enough to make me feel comfortable that there would still be money left after the people in front of me had gone. I couldn't help but size them up and try to gauge whether they looked like the kind of people who had a few hundred bucks in their account, or perhaps a hundred thousand. The latter of which would certainly leave me hung out to dry.

There was an awkward quiet among those of us on the line, which was unusual for the friendly community bank. A few of the customers seemed to have no idea what was going on.

"Man, I've never seen the bank so crowded," I heard someone utter as the tellers worked quickly in an attempt to keep the line flowing. Still, nobody who understood what was going on would spill the beans. Those of us who knew just wanted to get our cash and be on our way. Surprisingly, the man in front of me actually deposited money, and then it was my turn.

"Hello Ray," Theresa Hamill, a familiar bank teller said with a sigh conveying her sense of being overwhelmingly busy.

I took a deep breath of hope and handed over my withdrawal slip, only to see Theresa's eyes open wide at the figure in front of her. I had a lot of money in that bank, and I wanted it all.

She called over the bank manager, Lloyd Hassell, who also happened to be my boss. Lloyd was a kind fellow who ran the bank in a very conservative and responsible manner compared to other banks. Unfortunately for him, there would be no escaping this fateful day – not for the big city banks, not for the local small banks, not for anyone.

Theresa handed over the withdrawal and Lloyd looked at it, drawing his head back for a moment before looking at me quizzically. I maintained a deadly-serious expression before nodding in affirmation at my sincere wish to retrieve all of my money. He nodded back, almost in defeat, before retreating to the open safe.

As time went by and I waited patiently, the line continued to lengthen behind me. People remained generally silent, but a small buzz was beginning to pick up. Finally, Lloyd returned from the safe, motioning for me to come to his office. I did.

Amazingly, it turned out that luck was in my favor yet again, because I withdrew every last cent that bank had. I was almost able to liquidate my entire account, but the bank was a few hundred short. Lloyd could only shrug and hand over the sack of cash, which he placed in an ordinary looking paper shopping bag.

"Sorry Lloyd," I said. "I have to protect my family."

"No hard feelings," he responded glumly. "If it wasn't you, it would be the guy in line behind you. I'll give you a moment to get out of here, and then I'll close the windows."

"Besides," I added. "I know how you run this place, and if any bank in the country is going to survive this, it will certainly be this one."

"Let's just hope that *I* survive when I start telling my customers they can't have their money," Lloyd said, devoid of any jest in his tone. "Now why don't you head out the side-door."

Knowing that there were going to be a lot of very disappointed folks behind me in line, helping to sneak me out was a very kind gesture. It's a difficult thing being denied access to your own money from the bank. If people there knew I had mine, but they weren't getting theirs, it could make me a target even in a friendly town like Liberty Gulch. Lloyd realized this and was trying to protect me from a potential mob.

I slinked out the door quietly, just as Lloyd Hassel turned to the rest of his customers and began to explain that the bank vault was empty and that they would have to return another day.

I felt badly for Lloyd. How was the bank manager of the Liberty Gulch National Bank expected to be prepared for a run on his bank because a few foreign countries had a secret plan in place to usurp the currency? I felt bad for those in line behind me, too. Their deposits were insured, but not having access to your own money when you wanted it seemed like a horribly concerning position.

As I headed back to my truck, I could hear some raised voices in protest from inside the bank.

I walked briskly, knowing that I didn't want to be identified as the man who took all the cash from the bank's safe. What I didn't know at that time, was that it would also be my last day of employment at Liberty Gulch National Bank.

CHAPTER EIGHT

I exited the parking lot trying to act as normal as possible as cars filled with unlucky depositors began pouring in. Looking down at the bag sitting in the passenger side seat, I was thankful for having made it to the bank in time to secure the bulk of our life savings.

I couldn't imagine the scene that must be transpiring at banks across the country, especially in places where people were typically less cordial. If Liberty Gulch National Bank could experience a bank run, then *every* bank must be having a similar experience.

Even with the promise of FDIC insurance, the country wasn't prepared for an all-out, nationwide run on the banks. We had been lulled into thinking this was the case, but at that moment I knew that the country was in big trouble.

I tried to follow the potential line of events to stay out in front of whatever the next development might be. A large number of bank failures would cause a depletion of the FDIC's insurance fund. Once that fund was dry, insured deposits were backed by the U.S. government itself. In other words, it all just added to the national debt, which had already been growing at an unsustainable pace and was being supported by Federal Reserve money printing measures. With the dollar being pushed aside in international commerce in favor of the new Russian/Chinese currency, who would have the motivation to hold dollars anymore?

Once again I looked at the bag in the passenger seat, only this time, instead of thankfulness for having secured it, I worried that perhaps I should consider what might happen if the contents of that bag weren't worth as much tomorrow they were right now.

I was still angry at myself for succumbing to the popular belief that things were improving when I agreed with Charlotte that the two of us should return to work. I should have had the conviction to say, "I don't think this thing is over yet." But I didn't and it could have cost us our life savings. Now I was done with the guilt of feeling "paranoid." From now on, I was going to have conviction in my beliefs and take control over my decisions accordingly.

Before heading back home to let Charlotte know the good news, I decided to make one more stop. After leaving the parking area at the place of my employment, it was now time to pay a visit to Charlotte's.

Morris Roberts' Jewelers was located in the main shopping plaza in town, right across from the grocery store where Anna and I stocked up the other day. I was happy to have my bag of cash and thrilled it wasn't still sitting in the bank, but now I was nervous about whether or not the purchasing power of my stack would hold. I didn't really know much about investing in gold or silver, but what better way to kill two birds with one stone – I could insure myself against inflation while making a certain special someone very, very happy.

The bells that hung on the opposite side of the door chimed loudly as I entered. Not surprisingly, the store was completely empty when I entered, except for Charlotte's boss, Morris, who sat behind the counter looking through a loupe at some of his wares.

"Hey, Ray" he said with a smile. "Nice to see you."

Morris was an older gentleman in his late 70's. He sported a head of silvery-gray hair haloed around a substantial bald spot, and a well-kept beard that matched. Morris and his wife moved to the country from the big city a long time ago. He wanted to escape the hustle and bustle, just like we had. In that sense, we had a lot in common.

"How's business, Morris?" I asked.

"Pretty quiet," he admitted. "Everyone in town seems a little concerned lately, and I'm not quite sure I can blame them."

"Well, maybe I can help."

Sometimes when you're looking to make a large purchase, or in this case more of an investment, it would seem wise to hold your cards close to the vest. But Morris was a straight-shooter and a trusted family friend, so I just laid it out for him.

"Morris," I said, "I need to spend some money." With that, I took about half the stack of cash I had in the bag and laid it on the counter.

"I see."

Over the next fifteen minutes, Morris helped me find some of Charlotte's favorite pieces in the store. Having worked alongside her, he knew exactly which ones she coveted. I was looking primarily for items that would hold their value and was focused on the purity of the stones and the metal and less on the fancy artistry. Luckily, Charlotte had simple taste and most of her favorites fit that description.

When we hit the number I wanted to spend, Morris laid out all the pieces and I handed over the cash.

"You know," he said. "Ever since my wife passed, I've held onto this store and it has treated me well. She may not know it, but Charlotte helped me through a lot of that and I owe her a lot more than the salary she's been paid."

"Morris," I said. "She's enjoyed every moment of it. This job is exactly the reason we moved to Liberty Gulch."

"I know it," he said with a sigh. "But I'm getting older and it's just about time for this old man to call it quits."

I guess the thought sounded logical enough, and deep down we knew that the old man wouldn't live forever. But I knew Charlotte would be disappointed to hear it.

"I'm glad I could help you out," he continued, "but seeing this place in such disarray with gas prices and such, I think maybe I should head out of here sooner rather than later."

"Charlotte is going to be so disappointed," I said.

"I know, I know. That's why I want you to have these as well." He handed over a red velvet bag, shut tight at the top with a shoelace-type rope. I opened it, and slid out the contents – two rather large diamond earrings, a few gold bracelets with specks of jewels set in them, and a necklace with a large red stone dangling from it.

"Is this?" I began to ask picking up what looked like a man's gold ring.

"Yes," Morris said. "It's my wedding ring. When Louise passed, I wore it for a few weeks in her honor. But I found it was a constant reminder of how much I missed her, and I found myself sobbing every time I looked down on it – especially when I was in this store that we both built together."

"I can't take this," I insisted.

"Yes, you can," Art countered. "And you will. Don't think I haven't noticed you don't have a ring on that finger, Ray."

I looked down at my hand and the bare ring finger. It had been that way since the first summer we moved into our new home. The three of us had walked through the woods in search of the lake we knew was on our property out back. After a short walk we found it, and it was much bigger than we ever expected. It was a hot day and in an adventurous moment, we decided to strip to our underwear and go for a swim.

We stayed in that lake for hours splashing around and having a grand old time on a perfect summer day. Only, when we finally decided it was time to head back to the house, I realized there was one thing missing – my wedding ring.

I was extremely distraught at the time. When Charlotte put that ring on my finger years ago, I knew it would never come off. At least, that was my intention. But now it was somewhere at the bottom of the lake… lost forever.

I always meant to replace it, but just never got around to it. Besides, a replacement would never mean as much to me as the original.

"Try it on," Morris said.

I looked at him strangely. It felt so personal, almost like sharing someone's toothbrush, only without the germs. He picked up the ring and grabbed my hand, pushing the ring over my knuckles. It fit perfectly.

"There," he said. "It fits you better than it ever fit me."

I looked at my newly adorned finger. "It fits me better than my old ring fit me, too."

"There," Morris said conclusively. "It was like it was meant to be."

"But Morris," I observed. "I'm already married."

We both laughed heartily, which broke up what was an otherwise emotional moment.

"Morris," I began to ask, now turning my attention to the remaining items in the bag. "Is this stuff all real?"

"Yes," he said. "It's all real – the gold, the diamonds and even the ruby."

"I cannot accept all of this."

"Bullshit," he exclaimed. "This jewelry belonged to my wife."

"And it should stay with your family," I insisted.

"No," he said. "I loved this town and I loved running this store. I've spent more time here than anywhere else in my life. This place is where my real family is, and I'm more excited to give that bag to someone I know will appreciate it than to our bratty kids who won't even know it existed."

He shoved the bag over towards me in such a forceful manner that I knew there was no way I could say no.

"Besides," he continued. "I've been working in this business forever and we've done quite well for ourselves here. I've still got plenty to leave the kids. But, the stuff in that bag," he said as he lightly pounded his chest with his closed fist. "The stuff in that bag is what meant the most to me and I would be most grateful to know that it wound up somewhere it could be appreciated. I want Charlotte to have it."

"When are you leaving?" I asked. "Charlotte will surely want to thank you herself."

Morris grabbed the stack of money off the counter and held it in the air. "See this?" he asked.

I nodded.

"This was all the sign I needed. When a smart guy like you walks through my door and hands me over a stack of cash for jewelry, not only to make his wife happy but to protect his family against an economic collapse, then I think it's a sign. I'm going to pack this place up and leave tonight."

"Where will you go?" I asked.

"My son and daughter live in Virginia," he said. "When their Mom died, they asked me to come down and live with them. But I refused. I couldn't let go of the memories here. But now," he said, taking a deep breath before continuing. "Now, I can leave peacefully knowing that I made the right decision. I just hope I have enough gas to get there."

We both shared a sort-of forced laugh at that comment. I was truly sad to see the store close and Morris move on. Charlotte was going to be devastated when I told her, but this time around losing a job would feel a lot different. We were no longer dependent on our salaries to support a lifestyle, so there was no sense of desperation. Rather, it was simply sad that we were going to lose our friend and that Charlotte would not be able to go to a job which she truly enjoyed.

I spent a good deal of money that day, although in a way I didn't feel like I was spending it since I was buying something for investment purposes that I hoped would hold its value. The fact that Charlotte would be tickled pink to receive it was an added bonus.

I said goodbye to Morris, thanking him profusely and giving him a man-hug with a closed-fist, double-pat on the back of the shoulder. I had been there quite some time and knowing that I had left the house in such a rush, I was sure that Charlotte would be concerned by my prolonged absence. I jumped in the truck and headed back up the hill with a decent stack of cash and a bag full of jewelry.

As I swung by the bank, I could see that the scene there had only escalated. People were lined up outside the door, presumably waiting for their money. The police had been called and were trying their best to keep order, but it appeared to be a difficult task.

For once in my life, I felt lucky. I had hardly watched television in recent years, yet I just happened to catch an important story as it was reported. Following a hunch, I quickly made it to the bank just in time to withdraw all our cash there. Then I turned that cash into physical assets at opportune prices from a man who just happened to make a life-changing decision as I sat in his store.

As I looked at the crowd in front of the bank, I was thankful that I was not one of them. It was a very bad day for a lot of people. Many wore looks of desperation, their faces strewn with concern over the inability to get access to their own money.

What was going on here? What had happened to this place that seemed so very normal just a few days before? I flipped on my cellphone to look at the picture of Anna with the rainbow. What happened to *that* day? What happened to *that* moment, when everything seemed so perfect?

I could have never predicted these events occurring as they had these past few days. Of course, what I didn't understand then was that things were going to get even worse.

Returning home was certainly bittersweet. In a way I felt like a conquering hero, complete with a bag of of cash and another bag of jewelry. But seeing the desperation on the streets and knowing I would have to relay to Charlotte that Morris was closing the shop certainly brought down the mood. I half expected the girls would hear the truck coming up the driveway and meet me outside, like they often did. But they never appeared. Probably working away at some lesson in the playroom, I thought.

Even though we sent Anna to public school, when the system shut down for the summer Charlotte often assumed the role of teacher in order to keep Anna up-to-date on her lessons. We never understood the whole "summer vacation" aspect of public school and knew that it was to our detriment in our own experience. You never returned to school in September as sharp as you were when you left in June, and it always took some time to refresh your memory before picking up where you left off. It seemed such a waste, so to keep Anna sharp, we set up a little school-like area in her playroom and Charlotte performed her version of homeschooling. It seemed to work – especially in reading, where Anna was extremely advanced for her age.

Opening the door, I listened for Charlotte to call to me in the way she usually did. But it didn't come. Neither did Anna race her way across the kitchen floor to give me my traditional hug. I was beginning to grow a little concerned, especially after seeing the mayhem going on in town.

"Hey guys, are you here?" I called

"We're in here, Dad," responded Anna.

"Ray, you gotta come and see this," added Charlotte.

Happy to hear their voices, I casually threw my keys onto the kitchen island, and went in to see what was so important that they couldn't come and say hello. The two of them sat there on the floor, staring together at the television screen – a rare occurrence for this household. They were mesmerized, almost in a trancelike state.

When I looked at the screen, I understood why. I was shocked at what I saw.

The city was literally ablaze. Riots had broken out and it looked like the police had lost all control. Anna averted her gaze for the moment to acknowledge the presence of her father and provide me with an update.

"Daddy, we saw people dying."

CHAPTER NINE

After hearing those words come out of my innocent daughter's mouth, my attention focused on Charlotte, but she ignored me. There was a momentary lull before she just said, "Shhhhh," placing one finger over her mouth and using the other hand to wave me in.

Between scenes of violence and mayhem, newscasters filled us in on the details. The big city banks ran into the exact same problem as the one in Liberty Gulch. All of a sudden, everyone wanted their money and the banks didn't have it. People were up in arms and began protesting. As the number of protesters grew, their patience did not. Eventually, they snapped – glass windows were smashed, security guards were overpowered. They set fires and attacked bank employees.

Widespread panic erupted.

People were being shot in the street – which is exactly what Anna had seen right in front of her eyes on television. All that work I had done protecting her innocence after the night the police barged in was for naught.

While that was going on, gangs of looters began ransacking private residences and apartment buildings taking all they could. It was mass hysteria and the police simply could not be everywhere at once. The fires raged and the news crews were catching it all.

The mayor had been on TV telling everyone to calm down and stay in their homes, but that just seemed to make everyone panic all the more. The police began using force and once the shooting began, there was carnage on the streets; on live television. It was right there, in the place we left just a few years ago.

For a brief moment, I thought of my old boss Mort and my former co-workers and what they must be doing to ride out this storm. Were they still in the office? Had they rushed home to protect their families? What would I have done under those circumstances?

In the cities, mass transit had been the only form of travel over the past few weeks. Ever since gas prices had skyrocketed, cabs and cars had all but disappeared from the streets. But the rioters had taken over the major bus and train stations and all public transportation had now completely ceased. People were stuck in the city with no way to leave.

Then it turned more primal.

In times of trouble, people turn towards the bare necessities. In a hurricane or a blizzard or any type of emergency, the first thing people do is secure the things they need most. In this case, they turned to the supermarkets. Food prices had already been inching up due to the price increase in transport, but it had yet to become anything close to a crisis. I almost felt silly for stocking up as much as I did a few days ago, but that would quickly change.

The cameras cut to a restaurant where looters had broken in and were carting out trays of food. It was happening all over town. Grocery stores, delis, restaurants – anyplace that usually had food was looted by the hordes – people were frightened. If they couldn't get their money out of the bank, they might not be able to afford to eat, either. It had started with the banks, but had now spread to the food.

Martial law was eventually declared, but it seemed to have little effect. The National Guard was called in, but people were shooting at them from building windows and the soldiers were hesitant to fire back at private residences, not knowing if innocent civilians might be inside.

This went on for days and we watched, helplessly wondering what had become of the people we knew. In the end, thousands of American citizens would be killed in the streets. It would come to be known as The Food Riots, but to be sure, the violence all started with the failure of the banking system. And then, when people got desperate, they began to question where their next meal might come from and they did what only comes naturally.

They did what they needed to do in order to survive.

We felt relatively safe and secure being a few hundred miles away from the crime spree we were witnessing on television day after day. But we still stayed at the house, not even bothering to head into town and get the scoop from the locals on how The Food Riots were affecting the neighborhood.

The scene in the city was still tenuous at best. Residents and people who had been stuck there were clamoring for a means of escape, but were fearful of leaving their homes. The National Guard set up evacuation schedules, securing parts of the streets as exit-ways. Some people were lucky enough to have cars with enough gas in them to drive across bridges and through tunnels. But most of them walked.

You had to see it to believe it. It was a mass migration – the complete desertion of the big city. After a week of evacuations, there seemed to be nobody left. The National Guard exited the city as well because there were no more innocents to protect. The only people left were the rioters, the scoundrels, the thugs and the scavengers – living off what the once proud citizens of the city had left behind.

I was now happy that I had over-prepared for such a possibility. We had enough food for months, possibly a year if need be. Occasionally, I got out of the house to harvest my garden, which was a decent size now that I had the space in the backyard. Never did I expect we would have to rely on it for survival, but I was happy that it existed.

We sat glued to the television for most of those days. But one day there was an unexpected knock on the door.

Generally speaking, people were friendly in the country, and often times someone from around the neighborhood would come knocking. It wasn't a new thing to get a visitor, though with what was going on in the world, it did give me a brief moment of angst. When I thought about it, it was a little disconcerting. People around the country were desperate for food too, and I had plenty.

I went to the door feeling a little more alert to potential danger than I normally would, but as I approached, my fears dissipated with the appearance of a friendly face.

Mitch Russell was an old friend from high school whom I had kept in touch with for quite some time – at least, until we moved up to the country. We used to go bar-hopping when we all lived in the city during happier times. He was my wingman the night I met

Charlotte – "taking one for the team," as they say, when Charlotte's less attractive friend began meddling in what was a budding relationship.

For the most part we had kept in touch via e-mail and social networking. But still, I was very surprised to see him standing at my door.

"Mitch," I said with a note of shock.

"I know," he answered. "You're surprised to see me."

"Yeah, I am… but you're welcome here anytime. Come in, come in," I said, holding the door open. "How the hell did you get here?"

Before breaching the threshold of the door, Mitch turned and pointed towards the driveway. "On that."

There in the driveway was a bicycle. It was no ordinary bike and you could tell right away it was designed for racing. "Are you kidding?" I asked. "It's gotta be 400 miles from here!"

"Sounds about right," Mitch admitted. Over the past few years, he had taken to cycling and gotten himself in amazing shape. I hadn't seen him in so long that I nearly forgot about his passion for the sport, but looking at that space-age bike was proof that it had not been a passing fancy. When I thought about it, I knew he had been on rides of 100 or more miles in the past, so maybe it wasn't such a surprise that he could make it this far.

"Well then, what took you so long?"

Removing his backpack from his shoulder, Mitch flung it on the ground and turned again to face the street. Pointing towards the road, he noted, "Because I had to wait for that."

In the distance, just cresting the hill, I could barely make out a figure bobbing up and down, pedaling a mountain bike. He wasn't having an easy go of it, and for the briefest moment it looked like he might fall over in defeat. But he kept on going and as he got closer I started to get a better picture of who it was.

Jimmy Fogg was another friend from my high school days who lived in the city as well. He was stocky and a little more lumbering than Mitch and it showed as he dumped his bicycle on the ground and collapsed in the shade of the big oak tree.

"He's such a pussy," said Mitch. "I've been dragging him around for the last few days. I would have made it here in half the time if it wasn't for him."

We walked over to where Jimmy had taken his place underneath the shady tree and watched as he panted and wheezed. As we approached him, I could tell that his t-shirt was soaked through with sweat. Mitch was wearing a cycling shirt and looked like he had barely broken one.

"Jimmy?" I asked.

He rolled over on his side, facing away from me while he continued to try to catch his breath. Flinging his hand in the air, he made a poor effort at a wave hello. I grabbed onto the hand and tried to pull him up, but he was just dead weight and fell back into a heap causing Mitch and I to emit a hearty chuckle.

Finally, he dragged himself up to his knees and began to explain between deep breaths. "I've been riding this shitbox mountain bike for days while he's driving that spaceship thing," he said pointing towards Mitch's high-tech racing bike. "And this hill. Who the fuck buys a house on a hill like this?"

His agony fed our laughter and the two of us cackled as Jimmy gathered himself, stood up, and walked toward the house. Dismissing us with a wave of his hand, he walked right up to the front door as if he had lived in the house for years. He took off the backpack and said, "I've been on that bike for days and my ass is killing me. Some of us can take shits in the woods comfortably, but not me. Ray, it's good to see you but I have to go blow up your bathroom." And with that, he stormed inside the house.

I picked the bike up off the ground and Mitch and I wheeled them both into the garage and parked them inside. It was shocking to see my two old friends at my front doorstep and the method they had chosen to get there. The Food Riots must have been even worse than I thought and I couldn't wait to hear their story.

It never occurred to me that old friends might seek solace from the riots by riding bicycles to my house, but it gave me a sense of value to know that they would seek me out in a time of need. I knew the riots were bad and I feared that old friends and colleagues might be in danger. Cell phone connections were sporadic at best as the towers were overburdened with calls. We walked back up through the front door and turned right into Anna's playroom where her mother was teaching her some math.

"Was that Foggdog who just went barreling through the house like a ball of fire?" Charlotte asked.

Jimmy Fogg's nickname, "Foggdog," arose from the incredible

way he used to offend women in the nightclubs of the city. His technique was anything but subtle and he had an amazing way of accepting rejection and moving on. He was an aspiring womanizer, and we all enjoyed watching him in action. Over time, he embraced the name and happily owned it.

"Yeah, that was him," I confirmed. "Do you believe these two rode bicycles all the way up here from the city?"

Charlotte was happy to see our old friends amidst the chaos, and she walked over to greet our new guests – well, at least the one who wasn't in immediate need of the rest room.

"We have two extra bedrooms and you guys are welcome to stay as long as you wish," she said while giving Mitch a friendly embrace.

"We just wanted someplace safe to go for the time being," Mitch said. "We don't have family in the area and, well, we couldn't exactly ride the bikes down to Boca Raton. Well, I take that back. I could ride to Boca Raton, but *this guy*," he said as he pointed up towards the stairs Foggdog had just ascended.

Once the energy of their arrival died down and our two guests showered and changed, we all sat down around a table to eat. For me, it was a happy moment amongst recent tension and confusion. There is something about the company of lifelong friends that allows one to escape the seriousness of the time and enjoy the moment at hand.

"You boys must be famished," Charlotte observed.

"Yes, yes I am," Foggdog said, as he began tearing into the food laid out before him.

I had taken out some steaks from the freezer downstairs and I figured that now was as good a time as any to throw them on the outdoor grill. Baked potatoes accompanied the steaks along with some grilled zucchini with balsamic vinegar that came from the garden out back.

Foggdog tore into the steak like he hadn't eaten in months, while Mitch proceeded in a much more mannerly fashion and started to tell us the story of how they escaped the city.

"The riots had been going on for a few days and I was hunkered down in my apartment when Foggdog came to my door at about four in the morning, wearing all black and carrying a backpack. The rioters were going door-to-door in his neighborhood, so he hid in an alley and waited until dark before finding his way uptown to my place."

Foggdog wasn't even looking up as Mitch told his story – he just kept attacking the food.

"The evacuation route was set up the following day, and I wasn't so sure that I wanted to leave. There wasn't any place for me to go. That night the two of us emptied out my liquor cabinet and the thought just hit us: we could come here. We tried to call you, but the cell phones weren't working."

I waved off his apology for not calling in advance. I just wanted to hear the rest of the story.

"I knew I could make the ride, but wasn't sure Foggdog was going to be able to keep up. I had my racing bike, which I use every day and I had seen a mountain bike locked up in the basement of the building a while back. So, after drinking the rest of my liquor, we decided to steal the bike. It's not something that I would normally do, but the riots were a horrifying experience to live through. I thought there was a good chance that whoever left the bike had either escaped the city already, or had other means of transportation. At least, that's how I justified it.

"So, we went down there and, as luck would have it, the bike was completely unlocked. It was as if they left it there for us. The first thing we did the next morning when we heard the evacuation crews setting up, was grab the bike and head out.

"We knew we couldn't bring a ton of supplies, so we packed light – only things that were absolutely necessary. I left a lot of things behind... we both did. But we got ahead of the pack and were amongst the first to get over the bridge that morning. We were surrounded by well-armed military men who carved out safe areas in the roadways so that we wouldn't get fired upon.

"We crossed the bridge fairly quickly and made it safely to the other side. We stopped there to take a moment to say goodbye to the city we called home for all those years. But when we turned around, what we saw was completely unrecognizable. There were fires all over town, smoke trails laced into the sky. Military helicopters flew between the smoke trails searching for trouble spots. It was an intense sight; one I'll never forget."

"Charlotte," Foggdog interrupted. "Can you pass the barbecue sauce?"

Charlotte rolled her eyes as she passed the sauce and watched as

Foggdog globbed a whole bunch of it over the steak and continued to eat.

Mitch laughed under his breath and shook his head before continuing his story.

"Once we were over the bridge, we thought the hard part was over. We knew the direction we wanted to travel to get here, but the only way we knew was the highways. It turned out that was fine because there wasn't very much traffic – nobody can afford the gas and once we got far enough away from the city, actually seeing a car became a rare occurrence.

"In the beginning, we were naïve. We just assumed everyone on the road was in the same boat. This was not the case – a lot of the cars that were on the road were stolen and their passengers were more like pirates than travelers.

"We were riding down the street and Jimmy was about fifty yards behind me, trying to keep up."

"I had a fucking mountain bike," he protested.

"Hey!" I interjected. "Please watch the mouth in front of Anna."

Cursing was really nothing new to Anna, but I was just a little put off at Foggdog's carelessness and needed to remind him that he was now in the presence of our child and that he would need to watch his mouth. He shot a guilty look my way, but then just continued to eat.

Mitch continued. "The first time, the car pulled up right in front of Jimmy's bike. I heard the tires screech and quickly rode back as three men, two of them brandishing knives, jumped out of the car to attack. They wanted his backpack, but that wasn't going to happen."

"How did you get rid of them?" I asked, dying to hear how the story ended.

"I just showed them this," Mitch said, revealing a handgun that had been attached to his hip.

"I coulda handled them," Jimmy shot back, with a mouthful of steak. "Anyone going to eat this?" he asked, pointing to an extra baked potato on the serving tray. He didn't even wait for an answer, he just took the potato and started buttering it up.

"Really?" Mitch asked. "Are you going to even take a breath?"

"Do you know how many miles we just rode to get here?" Jimmy asked, his mouth still full. "I need to refuel."

We all just shook our heads and tried to stay out of his way.

"There were a couple of close calls like that on the way up. The last one wasn't even that far from here – musta been within 20 miles or so. We tried to avoid people as best we could, but people out there are getting desperate. They're hungry and there's no food anywhere. The restaurants, the grocery stores, the convenience marts – they're all closed."

"Well," I offered, "we have a decent supply of food up here. You guys are welcome to stay as long as you like."

"Thanks," Mitch said appreciatively.

"Yeah, danks," Jimmy added, the food in his craw getting in the way of clear speech.

"I have a bad feeling about this whole thing," Mitch explained. "The city is in pieces and who knows when people are going to be able to go back. The economy has been crushed and with gas prices as they are, I don't know when the distribution channels will be up and running again. I'm really concerned this could get way worse."

"*Worse?*" Charlotte chimed in. "How can it get much worse?"

"Well, the government is on its heels and can't keep up with all the work they need to do. The economy is dead, at least temporarily. The banks are closed, gas is too expensive, and we have no way of knowing whether or not things will ever return to normal. The violence in the city was… it was awful. It may only deteriorate, and if that happens, then all bets are off. It's going to be like Mad Max out there."

"Beyond Thunderdome?" Foggdog asked, followed by his impersonation of the film. "Two men enter, one man leaves. Two men enter, one man leaves. Two men enter, one man leaves." He continued saying it over and over in a grumbling voice, but we tried our best to ignore him and I offered Mitch my plan.

"We can be self-sufficient here," I said.

"In my gut, that's what I was hoping," Mitch said. "But I don't want to be a burden."

"Oh, no. I'm glad you guys are here. I could use the help."

"Two men enter, one man leaves. Two men enter, one man leaves," he continued, to the delight of Anna, who giggled louder and louder the more he said it. With his 8-year old audience soaking up his act, it only fueled Foggdog on and on until finally the rest of us had enough.

Mitch, Charlotte and I all looked at each other, then in concert we all pleaded, "SHUT UP!!!"

He did. And we quietly ate the rest of our meal and thought about the future. I knew things were bad, but it felt like we were somewhat secluded from the violence up here. Regardless, I was honestly glad they were here, even though Foggdog wasn't acting with the seriousness that the rest of us were. In times of distress, it's always comforting to have friends around.

Foggdog went to bed shortly after dinner. It was still early in the evening, but I could sympathize with his desire for sleep. They had ridden for hundreds of miles, down dangerous roads and up steep hills, sleeping on the side of the road whenever they got tired and eating very little along the way. Mitch was used to riding, but Jimmy Fogg was not and it showed.

Charlotte put Anna to bed and Mitch and I continued to talk. Only then did he reveal the true devastation and violence he had witnessed.

"You don't understand, Ray," he began. "The violence is something I had never seen before. Shootings, stabbings, beatings, rapes, violent mobs, you name it. I never thought I would see this happen in our lifetimes. We saw dozens of bodies on the side of the road the past few days."

It was clear he didn't want to startle Anna or Charlotte with the most frightening details of his experience. But over the next few minutes, Mitch detailed a number of the violent episodes he'd witnessed. After hearing these stories I was shocked the two of them had been able to make it out unscathed.

"This thing isn't just going to pass over in a few weeks and then return to normal, is it?" I asked, somewhat rhetorically.

"I don't see how it could," Mitch responded.

CHAPTER TEN

Over the next few days we largely spent our time glued to the television getting all the latest developments. The newscasts showed continued signs of struggle and hunger across the country, but especially closer to the cities as people were fighting over the last scraps of available food.

An obvious dynamic was slowly unfolding – the desperate and hungry were branching out from the cities and looting private homes in the suburbs. The police were outnumbered and instead of finding and bringing down the perpetrators of violence, they took defensive positions around the wealthier and more prosperous neighborhoods. It wasn't spelled out as such on the news, but you could tell from the reports.

"They're protecting their friends," Mitch would grumble. He was right, they were.

The super-wealthy were long gone, having flown out on their private helicopters or jets or sped away on their yachts to their homes overseas. It was interesting to see how the wealthy milked the middle class and the freedoms offered in their home country and then, when their resources were really needed to help solve a crisis, they fled. The wealthiest of the remaining lot had no place or no means of escape, so they hunkered down in their gated communities and arranged for around the clock police protection. The police were now more like a private security company, protecting the few who had assets that could be exchanged for protection.

After a little over a week, we finally decided to head back into town and see what was going on. The newscasts had only been covering events in the larger population centers, but the reality of what was going on in Liberty Gulch had completely escaped us. Besides, Mitch and Foggdog hadn't really seen the town other than during their bicycle ride on their way up the hill, so we thought it was about time.

The five of us squeezed into the truck and headed out. It was a calm, cool summer day – not too hot, but plenty of sunshine. It was the type of day one would really enjoy if things were normal. But with things the way they were, the beautiful weather went largely unnoticed. As we descended the hill, the complete absence of any other vehicle on the road was noticeable. Entering town, a large sign on the pumps at Art Brady's station read, "Sorry, No Gas Here."

The lack of gasoline really put a stop to people's lives. This was especially true in the country where manual forms of transportation like bicycles or walking weren't a convenient option given the much longer traveling distances.

If the gas station being closed was a surprise, what we found in town was completely shocking. As we made the turn down the main drag, we saw the library standing tall in the main intersection. We rolled past through the empty streets, noting the eerie silence. On the right, the parking lot to the grocery store was empty. The windows of the building were shattered and looking through, you could tell the place had been completely ransacked.

The shopping center across the way was similarly trashed, including Morris's jewelry store where Charlotte had worked and where just a few weeks ago I turned half of our checking account into a stash of treasure. I couldn't help but wonder if Morris had made it out unharmed.

I wanted answers to these questions, but the town seemed abandoned. The truck inched forward at slow speed as we took in the scene before us. Past the stores was the town church where many locals were parishioners. The doors to the church stood open and a sign read "All Food Donations Welcome." I could see movement inside the church and though I was curious, I dared not stop. Although the people of Liberty Gulch were always quite kind, the evidence of destruction in town was all I needed to see to stay wary. People in desperate need of things like food can sometimes do things they wouldn't normally do.

Perhaps it was naïve of me to think we could just drive right through town as if nothing bad was happening in the world. I felt as though driving down the main drag under these conditions exposed us somehow – perhaps making us targets. It wasn't a fear I had ever felt before – like that of losing my job and not knowing what the future might hold. It was much more raw – the fear of being followed or hunted, of being at the whim of bandits, looters and thugs. Maybe this was the same feeling Mitch and Foggdog had experienced on their bike ride escape from the city.

I couldn't believe what I was seeing. It happened faster than I had ever expected: the Food Riots had made their way to Liberty Gulch.

On the way out of town, I paid special attention to the Liberty Gulch Public Library. Unlike the rest of town, the building was surprisingly untouched, though I guessed looters probably wouldn't see much value in stealing books. It was normal working hours for the library, but the lights were out and it was fairly obvious that the place was closed. For a moment I wondered when it would open again. Then again, who knew *if* it would ever open again?

Pulling the truck out of the library parking lot, we decided it best to just head back towards home. At the corner, I noticed something that looked a little off – Art Brady's gas station looked untouched. The glass was all in place and the pumps looked as they always had – a little worse for wear, but not harmed in any way.

How could this be? Even if there were no gas in the pumps, surely the looters would have gone after what was inside.

"Sorry guys, I have one more stop," I commented as I pulled the truck into the makeshift parking lot, the loose gravel under the truck's wheels making that familiar popping noise it makes when riding over the tiny rocks. "Mitch, come with me. Foggdog, stay here." Mitch never went anywhere without his handgun and I knew he had it on him. Not knowing what we would find at the gas station, I thought we might need it.

We got out of the truck and cautiously approached the store's entrance. The lights were on, but the shelves were empty. That was really no surprise – any sort of food product would have been sold or stolen long ago. But it still didn't explain the lack of broken glass and signs of mischief.

I held my hand to the glass and peered through the window. Mitch stood off to the side, his hand near his hip where the gun was holstered and concealed. Peering around the store, there was nothing that caught the eye – no movement and nothing strangely out of place. I tried the door, but it was locked. So I knocked.

We waited a moment, but there was no answer. Nothing. Not one bit of movement inside and the only noise we heard was the gravel underneath our footsteps. I was just about to give up when I heard the unmistakable sound of a rifle pumping and a usually friendly, familiar voice speaking in a threatening tone.

"What do you think you're doing here?" Art growled after silently stepping out from the opposite side of the store.

Mitch took a step back. I sensed he might reach for the gun and for a second I feared the worst. But he stayed firm and I put my hands up and said, "Art, it's just me, Art. It's Ray."

"You're friend here's packin'," he observantly noted.

"Yes, yes he is," I admitted. "We were just passing through and couldn't believe the damage in town. Yet the gas station seems untouched."

"I guess now we know why," Mitch said referring to the armed Art Brady, still pointing the gun at us, though in a less threatening fashion.

Brady chuckled, and brought the gun down the rest of the way. "I'm sorry, fellas. I didn't recognize you. There's been a lot of trouble in town lately. People are hungry and desperate and they'll do just about anything for some food."

"I didn't realize it got this bad so quickly," I said. "At least, not until we came down here."

"They came in as a pack – on motorcycles mostly, but some cars too. They busted up every store, took everything they could. They came right through here and tried to use the pumps, but there hasn't been gas here for a while. Even at that price," he said, pointing up to the board that registered the last price of gas before supply ran out. "People used it all up and new deliveries have all been cancelled.

Anyway, I stood in the window here with my gun and they took heed and quickly moved on. I don't think many people in town were armed. At least, not by the look of things. And I don't think the police are even around anymore. Haven't seen a police car in over a week."

I couldn't believe what I was hearing. It was just a short time ago when I pulled into this gas station and paid four bucks a gallon.

Now, everything had changed. Everything.

Art continued. "It's amazing how quickly the food supply is running out. A lot of people seem to be getting skinny real fast. Many of them are holed up in that church, but they're running out of food there, too. More and more people show up at the church every day, but less and less food is making its way through that door."

It was heartbreaking to think of normal folks starving because the food had no way of getting here and they were unprepared to face this situation. I felt lucky that I had filled the cabinets, the pantry, and the meat freezer, not to mention cultivating the garden out back.

"How are you doing, Art?" I asked. "You hanging in there?"

"So far, I'm doing ok," he answered. "Got a good supply at home, but I may have to start huntin' again before too long," he said as he patted his gun.

There was a brief moment of quiet as the conversation stalemated in a sort-of uneasy concern for the situation everyone was facing. But the silence was short-lived, interrupted by the sudden sounds of motorcycle engines racing in the background. We all turned to face the deafening roar of three bikes making their way up the road from out-of-town. They briefly slowed down in front of the station as the gruff looking men aboard them turned their heads toward us.

We were about 20 feet from the truck and I briefly feared for Charlotte and Anna's well-being, but dared not move towards them and show weakness by revealing I had something to protect. At the sight of Art's gun readily at hand, and further deterred by the "No Gas Here" sign, the men decided to move on.

Strangely, instead of driving through town, the riders decided to turn off the main drag and onto the road that led up to our house. Just a few weeks ago, I would have thought nothing of it. But the very sight of these men racing up the hill towards my now vacant home, even though there were plenty of homes between here and there, made me fear the worst. There was a lot we had to protect up there – perhaps our very own survival. Apparently Mitch had the same premonition and we raced back to the car.

"Go get 'em," I heard Art say from behind us.

I liked Art Brady and was glad to see his store was still standing. Just a few weeks ago, Art would have taken his gun and hopped in the truck bed to help us deal with the bad guys, if indeed they were bad guys. But he had his own property to protect and his own safety to worry about. He stayed behind, and for a moment I couldn't help but wonder if the fabric of the people of Liberty Gulch was beginning to tear, just like some of the buildings in town.

Cursing myself at the stupidity of leaving the house unguarded, I raced the truck up the road after the three bikers, but there was no real chance of catching up to them. We glanced at each home we passed, hoping to see the men harmlessly dismounting their bikes, perhaps enjoying a laugh after a nice ride. My senses were telling me otherwise.

We rode up the hill and as the houses and turns went by, there were still no signs of the riders. My nerves grew with each passing house until ours was the only one remaining.

"I'm pulling in here," I told the rest of my passengers as I veered the truck off the road into a driveway of one of our neighbors, not caring at all whether or not they were home. "Charlotte, stay here with Anna."

Charlotte nodded while Mitch, Foggdog and I got out of the truck. I wasn't sure that this was the right move, but if there were three riders, I felt much more comfortable confronting them with three men. Charlotte and Anna would remain safe in the car; at least safer than they would be if they came along with us.

As we left I could barely make out Charlotte's voice. "Good luck," she whispered nervously. I was hoping we wouldn't need it.

Our house was just about a couple hundred yards up the road. As we walked along the curb, I could see the top of the old oak tree marking the entrance to the driveway, revealing itself more and more with each step. I was hoping that somehow we had missed them. Maybe we just hadn't seen them turn off the road. But as the driveway and the garage slowly came into sight, there was evidence to the contrary. Three bikes were parked non-discretely for the world to see, right in front of the garage.

"Ah, shit," Foggdog said, pretty much echoing the sentiments of all of us. "What are we going to do?"

"We can't let them steal the food or the supplies," Mitch said sternly. I was concerned even more so because it wasn't just the food, the gasoline tanks, and the tools we had in the garage that were so valuable – but our life savings and all that jewelry were sitting in a safe in the basement.

If the contents of the house were stolen, we would all be screwed.

Perhaps tomorrow we would be sitting in the church along with all those other hungry citizens of Liberty Gulch hoping for some food handouts. At the moment, I felt lucky we had caught these guys in the act. But as we took each step closer and closer to the house, that lucky feeling turned more and more into fear of the inevitable confrontation.

Calling the police wasn't even considered an option. Sitting at the busiest intersection in Liberty Gulch, Art Brady hadn't seen a police car in over a week. Even if we could get through to them on the cell phone, which only worked sporadically, we had no confidence that an officer would be able to make it here before the riders were finished looting the house.

We walked more cautiously now, not wanting to be seen or heard by the trespassers. There was a light breeze in the air that caused the trees to rustle, helping to cover the light sound of our footsteps.

"You have your gun?" I asked Mitch.

"Of course," he whispered.

"Maybe you should draw it now," I said. "No need to wait this time, I think we know what we're up against."

"Good idea." He drew the gun.

As we reached the oak tree, I could see that the doors to the garage were open and we could hear a commotion inside. As quickly and as quietly as we could, we ran to the garage and took a position near the doors. I stood next to Mitch, his gun drawn. On the other side, Foggdog stood brandishing a large stick he had found on the walk up the road. I placed my hand near my hip as if there were a gun there but, of course, there was not. I didn't think it would fake them out, but I figured that if it caused them a moment of hesitancy to think I was pulling a gun, it might be all Mitch needed to get off an extra shot if need be.

To say we took the men by surprise would be an understatement. All three were laughing joyously at their haul, which consisted of six one-gallon gas containers. Each had their hands full, which put them at an extreme disadvantage. They weren't the brightest of thieves, that's for sure.

All six of the containers abruptly hit the floor as Mitch yelled, "FREEZE!" and pointed the gun right at the would-be thieves.

Their hands hit the air in fear and they knew right away that they were now at the mercy of their captors. Unfortunately, none of us had any experience in situations like this and there was a momentary silence in the air. I didn't want them to sense any note of fear from us, so I took the reins.

"Get up against the wall," I yelled. The men immediately did as they were told. Mitch held his weapon steady and Foggdog held his stick in a threatening fashion. We didn't have much experience at this type of confrontation, but when you believe your life could be on the line, it's amazing the things you can do.

One by one, I frisked them, coming up with a few pocket knives, but no guns.

"What are you doing up here?" I demanded.

The man on the far left, a burly fellow with dark shades, a leather vest and black turtleshell helmet, was their spokesman. "We were just looking for some gas for the bikes and then we were on our way," he volunteered.

"Bull shit," I challenged, knowing full well that had we not shown up in time they would have certainly cleared the house of all useful tools, food, and possibly even the safe with all our cash and most of the jewelry I had purchased just a few short weeks before.

"No, really," the man continued. "The bikes are all on empty and there's no gas available anywhere. We're not thieves, I swear. We came up this way by accident. We were lost and didn't even know where we were going. We came to the dead end, saw your garage, and thought that it was our best chance."

Among us, Mitch had the most experience with bikes, including motorcycles. We made eye contact and both nodded. I walked over and took his gun from him, keeping it trained on our temporary hostages. I had never shot a gun before, but this wasn't time for me to start asking questions. So I pointed the barrel at the men as Mitch went over to the bikes.

"If those bikes aren't all on empty, you boys are really fucked," I threatened.

The men stood silently and seemed somewhat at ease even though they were being held at gunpoint after getting caught stealing red-handed. Mitch checked the three bikes and then looked over at me, shrugged his shoulders and nodded.

"They're all empty," he said.

This seemed like good news in that at least their story was honest.

"We're not thieves," the spokesman offered again, despite the six gas containers still sitting on the ground nearby.

"Do they have enough gas to get out of town?" I asked Mitch.

"No. Probably wouldn't even make it down the hill unless they coasted."

This was a bit of a conundrum – what were we going to do with these guys? I couldn't call the cops – nobody would come. I couldn't hold them captive – we didn't have the capacity or the inclination to feed and house three unknown men. Even if I let them go, they weren't going to get very far. The delay in my decision-making was beginning to raise the level of tension. Mitch and Foggdog had given up control of the situation and it was clear that this decision was now mine; though I wasn't sure I wanted it.

There was only one good option.

"Ok," I said. "Hands down and turn around. " They did as they were told. "Each of you take a gallon, but no more, then get the hell out of here and never come back."

Mitch looked at me with a sort-of defeated air of approval. We had no other choice. It felt wrong not to punish the thieves and it hurt to lose the gasoline supply. But without a police presence, there were just no other options.

Each man lifted a can of gas off the ground and took it to his bike. They filled them quickly and then started them up, the engines emitting a deafening roar. I kept the gun trained on them at all times, and just as they were about to leave, the leader turned to me.

"Thank you," he said. "You have been very generous."

I couldn't muster a "you're welcome," only a confident nod.

With that, the men rode away. I felt a sense of relief that they were gone, even at the expense of the three gallons of gas we just lost.

Just down the road, Charlotte and Anna had seen the riders go past and drove the truck back home. They were concerned about what had transpired, and seeing the bikers speed off offered no immediate relief. As they anxiously pulled into the driveway, they saw the three of us there next to the remaining three full gas containers. Unlike the greeting I received a few weeks ago after returning from the bank a conquering hero, this time I was barraged with a mighty double-bear hug. Little did we know that it wouldn't be the last time we'd be enjoying a thankful reunion after a harrowing, near-death experience.

After filling them in on the events, Charlotte was finally at ease. "I'm not worried about the three gallons of gas," she commented. "I'm just glad that everyone is safe. Besides, we have enough for now. By the time we're finished with it all, I'm sure Art's station will be up and running again."

Of course, that would prove to be wishful thinking.

CHAPTER ELEVEN

That night we sat at the dinner table, a little worse for wear after seeing the town in such disarray and experiencing the near robbery. The world seemed a more dangerous place now than it had when we woke up this morning.

"We need to have a plan," Charlotte observed.

Charlotte used to make fun of me for always trying to plan things ahead of time, but now it seemed of prime importance. Mitch agreed, though he appeared a bit subdued.

"What's the matter?" I asked.

He sighed, placing his fork down on the plate. "I shouldn't have come here," he said. "You were prepared for your family, but not for two stragglers. We are just going to be a burden."

With all the supplies in the house, I hadn't even thought it might come to something like that. Could we possibly run out of food? Maybe we'd put a big dent in our supply, but we were pretty well stocked and could probably last the whole winter if need be. I was confident that we'd somehow figure things out if it got further than that – be it farming or hunting.

"Mitch," I said. "If you can't turn to a friend in a time of need, then who can you turn to? You are here and you already helped us out once. What would I have done without a gun if those guys on the bikes just appeared at my house?" That realization seemed to make some sense to him as he nodded in agreement. "So, until this thing is over let's just consider you both permanent residents of this house."

"I won't let you down, Ray. I promise." He said it with such sincerity that I knew he would always be a great ally.

It was time to turn to more pressing issues. "I think the goal here needs to be self-sufficiency," I offered. "We need to be able to provide enough food for all of us and we need to make sure we can stay warm during the winter months."

"And we need to be able to protect ourselves against whatever might come up that hill," Charlotte offered.

Her point was well taken and I could tell that seeing three would-be biker thieves show up at our house had shaken her.

"I think we need to set a night watch," I said.

"No fucking way," chimed Foggdog.

"So you wouldn't mind sleeping in your bed one night and having guys break in and steal all our supplies?" I asked.

Foggdog's ulterior motive was apparent to us all. He was well known for his sleeping prowess and making him stand watch for a few hours at night would be torturous.

"I vote yes," Mitch agreed.

"I'll take a shift, too," Charlotte added.

Foggdog sat, looking defeated. "Fine," he capitulated without much objection before rising from the table and making his way to the living room as a juvenile form of protest. "Now I'm pulling guard duty," he mumbled on the way out. We just sat there and shook our heads. There was no time for petty protests – we were trying to evolve a plan for our survival.

"So – food, heat, and security are our top priorities. Let's discuss food first. This garden we have in the back has been a fun experience for me, but it was never meant to provide year-round sustenance. Our needs seem to have changed."

"Yes, I agree. So what do we do?" Mitch asked.

"Two things. First, we should expand this garden next year. In order to do that, we are going to need to cut down some trees at the edge of the forest to make room for more planting and more sunlight to get through. This is good though, because we're going to need a large supply of firewood for the winter. So we cut down a bunch of trees, clear the land, and stack the wood."

Mitch nodded, knowing that this meant we had a lot of work ahead of us.

"The other is that we have to start learning how to do a few things

– farming, trapping, hunting, treating illness and wounds, surviving – you name it. We're going to have to start researching, including how we're going to prep our plantings for next year. Every plant in that garden was bought as a seedling. Who knows if the garden stores will be open next year? We need to make sure we have seeds to plant. We're going to make sure we know how to kill and clean deer, rabbits, wild turkeys and stuff like that. We need to study up on survival."

"Eight years of undergraduate and graduate classes and not one mention of how to plant a fucking garden," Mitch signed. "And now that's the only thing I need to know."

"I have a feeling that we're going to learn an awful lot more about things we don't know as we go along," I admitted.

"Hey guys," Foggdog interrupted from the other room. "I think you should come in here and check this out."

Mitch and I looked at each other, immediately dismissing this request as something stupid. Ignoring the nuisance from the other room, we continued to sit at the table to plan.

But just as I was about to speak, Foggdog interrupted again. This time he walked back into the room to make sure he got his point across. "No, guys, for real. I'm not joking around. The President is going to speak in a few minutes. They interrupted all the TV stations – it sounds like it's pretty serious."

We decided to delay our plans for the moment and head into the living room. At this point, I don't think there was anything the President of the United States could do to help our situation. It was fairly clear that we were going to be on our own and we were now preparing for the situation as best we could.

We all gathered in front of the TV, and it was the President who kept us waiting another fifteen minutes before he spoke, which only frustrated us more. As always, his speech was long and tiring and could have been delivered in a few short sentences.

There was to be no relief in the gasoline situation and all price controls were being abandoned. Of course, there was no gas at the stations anyway so that didn't seem to matter. With the city now in shambles, markets were being opened over internet-based computer systems and were traded by a select few bankers and investment houses, where people were calling in to sell their stocks and bonds in an attempt to get cash. Of course, pretty much all of the banks were insolvent and the FDIC, along with the Treasury and the Federal Reserve were working feverishly to insure deposits and provide cash to those who wished to have it. This was an extremely slow process that would not be reconciled for a long period of time.

Domestic investors weren't the only ones desperate to sell their securities. Foreign holders of US debt were selling it like mad, causing a massive decrease in the value of the dollar in favor of the new currency. According to the President, it was a financial act of war. But it was left unclear as to whether there would be any repercussions for the offending countries in question.

With gasoline so expensive, it was difficult to secure imports. Domestic supply was becoming a very rare commodity. As valuable as it now was, gasoline was only being sent to government defense industries, the military, and those neighborhoods where citizens could afford obscene prices and police were available to protect it from thieves.

There would be no new supplies of gasoline for the remaining general public, including Liberty Gulch.

With no fix for the gasoline problem, there would be no easy fix to the food shortage and the developing hunger problems either. But the government wasn't going to sit by and do nothing, so they presented the people with a solution to their problem.

A number of large family and corporate farms across the country were being nationalized. Camps were being set up there to house anyone who showed up and needed food. If there was no way to get the food to the people, they would bring the people to the food. Each town would be designated a farm to report to and residents could board a scheduled shuttle that would bring them to where the food was, and they could stay until the problem subsided.

"Look, I know this is not the ideal solution. But people are hungry, and it is our responsibility to get them fed any way possible. As the situation returns to normal, people will return to their homes. America is not a country that lets her citizens go hungry. My Presidency will not be marked as the one that starved the American people. Rather, it will be the one that looked this desperate situation in the eye, and found solutions to the biggest problems she ever faced."

The nearest large farm to our area was about seventeen miles away, which meant it wasn't exactly walking distance. But it was fairly large and could probably feed thousands of people if necessary.

A secondary safety measure was put in place that allowed anyone reporting to the camps to delay their mortgage payments without penalty for as long as they stayed in the camps. With the banks insolvent, they didn't exactly have much in the way of argument to prevent this from being implemented. Either way, this last measure didn't affect us at all since we didn't have a mortgage to pay. But it turned out to be an incredible incentive for people to go to the camps, even if they weren't necessarily on the verge of starvation. There had been no official statistics released since the Food Riots began, but it was easy to see that a lot of folks had lost their jobs in the wake of it all and the last thing they wanted was to lose their homes as well.

I found myself asking aloud, "Would you ever imagine a day where the citizens of this country would need to become refugees in temporary camps just so they could get enough food to eat?"

Nobody answered, though eventually Foggdog would ask a silly question.

"So, what are we going to do?"

I wondered for a moment if he was serious, but the inquisitive look on his face indicated that indeed he was.

"What are we going to do?" I snapped back in a raised voice. "We are going to stay here and be resilient and take care of ourselves. Did you think we were going to be refugees?"

"Well, there's food there," he began to explain.

Mitch rolled his eyes and simply left the room. I could not be so forgiving.

"What do you think we were just discussing?"

"Yeah, but we don't have to worry about that anymore. We can just go down to the camp and wait it out with everyone else. Shouldn't we at least think about it?"

"Don't you have any pride?" I asked. "You can go to the camp if you like," I offered. "Either go with the rest of the needy, or stay here and work with the rest of us and earn your keep."

"Well, if you're going to put it that way," he said, "it's almost a no-brainer. Why slave away in the heat and be forced to play night watchman every night when we could go to the camp and have food and safety and sleep? Didn't you see those guys on the bikes? Next time, maybe they'll have guns."

"Fine. Go to the camp if you want. I'm staying here with my family. I knew you were weak, but I never thought you were such a pussy." The "p-word" raised the stakes somewhat, as it was a rarity for my vocabulary. I could tell it hit Foggdog in a spot that tested his manhood, but he didn't have a comeback.

I left the room in disgust, rejoining Mitch and Charlotte in the kitchen.

"I think he really might want to go to the camps," I reported.

"And you're surprised by this?" Mitch asked.

"What do you mean?"

"He's always been lazy, you know that. Food, sleep, and you know what else will be at the camp that won't be here? Girls!"

"Are you suggesting that he wants to go to the food camps because there are girls there?"

"Where else are they going to be? Not here."

I thought about it for a moment and it actually made some sense. "I guess there's a reason why we call him FoggDOG after all."

"No shit," Mitch agreed.

Liberty Gulch held a town meeting just two days later to discuss the procedures for reporting to the food camp. Foggdog and I rode bicycles down to the meeting, while Mitch, Charlotte and Anna stayed home. After the biker incident, we would never feel right about leaving the house unguarded. Someone always stayed behind, preferably armed in case of another incident.

The decision for me to go along with Foggdog on the trip was an easy one. Though he was the one reporting to the camp, I was the only person other than Charlotte who would be recognized as a resident of Liberty Gulch. We weren't necessarily low on gas in the truck quite yet, but who knew when we'd get a chance to refuel and at what price. Besides, I was still a little miffed at Foggdog for making me go through this ordeal, so even though I would have to pedal back up the hill as well, I knew he would especially hate being forced to do it. We hardly spoke on the trip down – I just couldn't believe that he was willing to give up his freedom just to meet girls and avoid a little hard work.

It was a nice summer day and coasting down the hill was very pleasant, though the awkward silence between us made it somewhat less enjoyable.

The gymnasium at Liberty Gulch High School was jam-packed. I didn't even think there were that many people in the town, but there they were. I recognized a number of faces, but ultimately I settled next to the friendly librarian.

"Hello, Mrs. Quigley," I said.

"Oh, hello," she responded with a smile which seemed to hide a bit of pain. I could see that she was notably thinner than the last time I saw her, which was just a few weeks earlier. She wasn't alone in this capacity – a lot of people seemed notably thinner.

"You know," I began, "I was at the library the other day and..."

"The library has been closed for a couple of weeks now," she interrupted. "And I'm not sure when it will open again."

"Then I'm going to owe a heckuva lot in late fees," I joked, resulting in a giggle from Mrs. Quigley.

"Are you going to the food camps?" I asked her.

"I don't see that I have much choice," she admitted. "My job is gone, I have no savings and I don't have the means to get my medicine and food. What about you?"

My heart felt for Mrs. Quigley, who was always so nice to Anna whenever we went to the library. I very badly wanted to offer her a spot in our house, but I wasn't sure that we were going to be able to sustain *ourselves* and I couldn't risk adding dependents. Besides, when I looked around and saw the number of friends of ours in same predicament as her, I knew that I couldn't hand out an invitation to everyone. I had to focus on my family and not being able to be more generous made me feel inconsequential and small. It felt selfish and terrible, but at least I knew she would be cared for and perhaps would put some of that healthy weight back on.

"No, we are staying behind. We think we can tough it out. But I brought my friend Jimmy down here because he decided to join you all."

I went to introduce Foggdog to Mrs. Quigley, but when I turned around he was gone. A few yards away I could see him already cozying up to a younger girl I recognized as Katie Marino, causing me to roll my eyes.

Mrs. Quigley had seen Foggdog come in with me and chuckled at my reaction to finding him talking up a younger woman. "That's Jimmy, I presume?" she asked.

"Yes," I said with a note of frustration and a sigh. "Yes, it is."

Mrs. Quigley quickly changed the subject. "I think I may have something for you," she said, searching her pockets before emerging with a keychain. She carefully pulled a key from it and handed it over.

"Take this," she whispered. "It's the key to the library. There is no alarm system even though it looks like there is one. Take care of the books for me while I'm gone. I'm not sure when I'll be back."

"But aren't you going to get in trouble for that?" I asked.

"What… for losing my key during the move?" she giggled. "Consider it a gift for Anna," she added. "You're going to need to keep her up on her reading and what is she going to do without access to a library?"

I was touched by her thoughtfulness and genuine care for Anna.

"Thank you, Mrs. Quigley. This is extremely gracious of you. We'll do the best we can to keep the place in good shape." I took the key from her and put it in my front pocket.

The crowd began to hush as the Mayor of Liberty Gulch took the stage. Mayor Carter had a rather meek personality, but had been in office for a couple of decades. Most elections he ran unopposed. People voted him in year-after-year because he was somewhat attentive to the town's problems and he rarely got in anyone's way. Of course, now that the town needed strong leadership, maybe he wasn't the best man for the job.

Mayor Carter tapped on the microphone before beginning. He spoke hesitantly and awkwardly for the next fifteen minutes or so, doing his best to give the details of the transfer to the food camp.

The government had nationalized Maly Farms, a corporate concern that was 17 miles from the center of the town of Liberty Gulch. Trailers and tents had been set up as temporary shelters to house thousands of local citizens from the neighboring communities. For many people, this was their only hope to get their hands on food and it seemed like most residents were preparing to take this option.

Once the random violence was back under control and gasoline prices returned to normal, a more cost-effective means of food distribution would be set-up, and then people would be free to return to their homes. He went on to detail the mortgage freeze program and what people needed to do in order to ensure they kept their homes. In many ways the food camp sounded like a really good deal.

The first bus would arrive tomorrow, making multiple trips back and forth until all registered persons were transported safely. This left many people with little time to make the decision as to whether to stay or go, but it seemed that most people were happy that they wouldn't have to wait very long to get to the food.

There were restrictions as to how much baggage people could bring and what type of things they could take with them. These were all detailed in a circulated handout.

Eventually, the speech ended and people immediately began to file out.

"Mrs. Quigley," I said. "Do you have enough to get you through the next few days?"

She blushed at my kindness. "Yes, I'll be fine. I had a brisket in the freezer and I was saving it in case things got really desperate. I think I'll be cooking that up today and it looks like I'll eat well until the bus comes."

That was certainly a bit of good news. The thought of this generous woman home alone going hungry was not very pleasant and I was glad she wasn't in desperation or pain. "Well, hurry back so Anna can tell you all about the books she read from your library." From there, we said goodbye, embraced, and went on our way.

I began to scan the crowd for Foggdog so we could get out of there and start pedaling back up the hill. As the crowd thinned, unsurprisingly he was nowhere to be found. Frustrated, I joined with the last remaining stragglers and headed out myself.

As I left the gymnasium I could see him across the parking lot, still talking to Katie Marino. I didn't know much about her other than her name and that her family consisted of her father Ed and a few brothers. She seemed to be in her late 20's or so, slender but muscular with long, curly brown hair and brown eyes. She was a good-looking girl and I wasn't shocked that Foggdog had singled her out.

I could see she was smiling and laughing as I approached. Foggdog must have been turning on the charm.

"Jimmy," I called. Using his nickname was something we typically did only amongst ourselves and it was considered in poor taste in the company of people who were not in our circle, especially if it was a girl he was putting the moves on.

Laughing, they turned towards me, Katie offering a warm greeting, "Hello, Mr. Stanton."

I wasn't much older than her, but people in this part of the country were always very polite and over time I got used to being called "Mister" or even "Sir."

"Hi, Katie. Nice to see you. Are you guys going to the camps?" I asked, somewhat surprised. Ed Marino always seemed like a tough-as-nails fellow, and I didn't think he would ever volunteer for something like this unless his situation was dire.

"No," she replied. "My Dad and my brothers would never allow it. We're going to give it a go on our own – my brothers are big hunters and we have a couple acres we can farm and about fifty chickens. I was just down here to say good-bye to a few of my friends."

"So was I," I said, making a slight dig at Foggdog.

"Sorry I ditched you, Ray," he said. "I saw that you found your friend so I just mingled with the crowd and met Katie," he responded. It took me a moment to figure out what he was up to, but then I got it. He dared not admit to Katie that he was going to the food camps, especially since she was strong enough to tough it out. Using the quick-thinking, manipulative ability only a pick-up artist could muster, he changed around the entire conversation to make it look as though we had come to the meeting so that I could say goodbye to Mrs. Quigley.

I couldn't help but sigh. In a way, I was frustrated at the dishonesty that came along with being friends with a horny, single guy. Then again, it felt a bit nostalgic from our old days in the city, and I followed my sigh with smile and a laugh.

Before leaving, Foggdog successfully came away with Katie's phone number. Then we hopped on our bikes, which seemed to be a popular mode of transportation these days just looking around the parking lot, and we were headed back up the hill.

"In case you didn't hear the Mayor, the bus leaves in two days, buddy," I advised my friend. "You're going to have to work pretty fast."

"No, I'm not," Foggdog said. "I changed my mind. I'm not going."

CHAPTER TWELVE

As the first buses in town were being loaded, Mitch and I stood in the backyard and hatched our plan for survival. The yard itself was a decent size for Anna to run around and play in, but it was by no means big enough for a garden to sustain us food-wise. Luckily, we owned acres of land surrounding the yard in every direction.

"It looks like we're gonna have to cut down some trees," I noted.

"Some trees?" Mitch asked. "We are going to have to cut down a lot of fucking trees."

He was right. Looking around, the woods were very dense, thick with shrubbery and trees – some areas thicker than others, but they stretched in all directions.

"Well," I remarked. "We're going to need a good supply of wood for the winter anyway, so maybe it's a blessing in disguise."

There was no time to waste and the two of us got right to work. For the next few weeks, days were relatively the same. A typical morning would find Anna and Charlotte harvesting the small garden we already had while Mitch and I cut down trees and remove their stumps. My truck proved useful in this task as we could chain it to the stump and rip it right from the ground.

Foggdog would generally stumble out in the late morning as Charlotte and Anna retreated to the house with their baskets full of vegetables so that Anna could start her lessons for the day. His job was to cut the trees we chopped down into firewood and then stack it neatly alongside the garage. He was fairly strong and wielded the axe effectively when he did so. But the work tired him out quickly and he took frequent breaks. On a number of occasions we found him down in the basement playing video games on an old Nintendo I had always had trouble throwing out because it never stopped working. When we chided him for his lackadaisical attitude, he would blow us off by suggesting we were paranoid and crazy and he was doing as much work as he could handle. For him, life returning to normal was a certainty. For us, we were not so sure.

Given what he had witnessed in traveling here, I was actually quite shocked at Foggdog's outlook. I surmised that he was in some sort of clinical denial, or perhaps he was truly affected by the images of death and destruction he had seen. Or perhaps it was something else.

When he wasn't working or down in the basement playing video games, Foggdog often made trips down the hill and into town, sometimes on the bicycle and occasionally even on foot. These trips were sporadic at first and then became more and more regular over time. He was typically pretty quiet about where he was going and what he was doing, but we all knew there was only one thing in the world that could motivate Foggdog to come up that hill time and time again. It had to be a girl.

Katie Marino was the girl in question, of course – the one he had met at the town meeting. Foggdog had begun seeing her, and over time their relationship grew. He was at least half a dozen years her senior, a figure that might have drawn a little scrutiny from Katie's father, Ed. But over time, Foggdog had a way about him that could win people over. It was a certain charm I guess you would say, and he must have done a good job on Ed Marino because whenever Foggdog had down time during the daylight, he was down the hill at the Marinos' house.

Sometimes, this wasn't such a bad thing because it gave us one less mouth to feed. As the afternoon waned into the evening, we would break for the day and come inside for dinner. I rationed food based on the belief that we would start to see crops in mid-summer of the next year or so, and there was plenty in our stores to last that long.

On a number of occasions a faction of us would head to town and, using Ms. Quigley's key, we'd go to the library. It was always somewhat dark in there and we never wanted to blow our cover by turning on the lights. Finding our way through the stacks with nothing but flashlights was certainly eerie, but the payoff was always well worth it.

Charlotte needed textbooks and homeschooling guides for Anna. The doors to the public school never opened that year. Anna needed reading material for her own enjoyment, and Mitch and I would gather up books on survival techniques including hunting and trapping, manuals on farming and agriculture, and medical journals. The best thing about bringing these books up to the house was that there were never any late fees.

Typically, after dinner we would cease working outside and begin to sort through the books for important lessons that would improve our survival skills. I truly believed that we would be fine up here in the house under the worst conditions. After all, didn't the pioneers head west with nothing on their backs? Didn't the American Indians thrive in these parts with no cell phones or electricity or plumbing or guns?

But I wasn't taught how to live this way. I was taught how to go to the office each day and peck away at a keyboard for hours while sitting in a chair. I bought my food and my clothing and paid my rent on time. I had a Master's degree, but none of those college courses taught me how to keep rabbits out of my garden or how to prepare seeds for the next year's planting. But the books did.

Fall faded into winter with a few dustings of snow and a slow transformation from bearable chill to crippling cold. Holidays came and went with less than the usual joy, but with an overabundance of thankfulness that we had done well to survive and prepare for the future.

Through months of hard work, the woods had been pushed back enough to give us plenty of open land to plant our crops come spring. We were hoping to become better hunters by then, too, or perhaps I should say trappers. The only shooting apparatus we had was Mitch's hand gun – not exactly a hunter's choice of weapon.

When the weather broke favorably, we would still get out and do some work. But the winter would prove to be harsh, and once we rolled into the new year we were largely relegated to indoors. Except Foggdog, of course, who would brave the blustery cold conditions to see Katie as often as he could. Having known him for so long, we rarely gave him a hard time about it. The fact that he would go out in the cold just to see her almost felt proof enough for us to believe that maybe, for once, our friend was beginning to enter into a real adult relationship.

My office had become quite a complete library, full of books borrowed using Mrs. Quigley's key. With the cold weather, we now had tons of time on our hands and reading tended to make us feel productive. Some days it felt like we barely spoke to one another – we just woke up, ate our meals and read our books.

Though I hadn't received a bill in months, the lights and the gas were both still working. With many of the utility employees either quitting or reporting to the food camps, the government nationalized the utilities and was running them with a bare-bones staff who we assumed had trouble enough keeping the lights on, making billing a secondary concern. I guessed that with so many people away at the camps, they weren't losing too much on the few people left behind. Besides, the banks were mostly closed and nobody was working anymore. Who possibly had the means to pay a bill? As such, brownouts were common, though they typically lasted only a few hours at a time.

Each time the power went off we would fire up the generator and make sure to plug in the freezer. Our meat supply was contingent on the freezer's ability to keep running, even as our gasoline supply was dwindling. At some point, I made the decision to focus on using up our meat stores – burgers, hot dogs, various cuts of beef, chicken and pork – so that if the power went out for an extended period and we ran out of gas, at least we'd still have our boxes of pasta and canned goods to keep us alive until summer.

Television continued to work, but many networks were looping reruns on auto-pilot or had shut-down altogether. For the most part, news networks would focus on giving broad "feel-good" reports of life at the food camps, which often had us questioning whether we had done the right thing by staying put. There were makeshift schools where kids were learning and outdoor sporting events when the weather cooperated. It almost looked like a party and though we could easily have made the choice to go and join them at any time, we continued to find pride in our ability to sustain ourselves.

While national news and coverage of the success of the food camps were plentiful, world news was certainly not. We were rarely brought up to date on anything about foreign affairs or the financial situation and whether or not global commerce was on the verge of recovery. Among those of us in the house, we took that to mean it wasn't going very well and there would not be a return to normalcy any time soon.

Local news was nearly non-existent, unless the networks happened to be at the nearest food camp. Other than that, the only local stories came in the form of weather forecasts, which were now done on a very broad basis. Local weathermen were a thing of the past and the national ones no longer approached their jobs with abundant jovial energy, but with a foreboding grimness of a person doing his job – nothing more, nothing less.

The forecast was typically bland, if not repetitive – every day of winter was "Possible Snow," but never any indication of how much. Some days we got an inch or two, sometimes four or five. Most days there was none at all. There was no way to tell what was coming, which is one of the reasons why the great January blizzard took us all by such great surprise.

CHAPTER THIRTEEN

We were all at home early that evening, except for Foggdog who had spent the earlier part of the day at Katie's house, as had become the usual practice. We liked to keep tabs on him so we knew whether or not we would have his help on the night watch and he typically called to check-in.

Foggdog would always time his return home just as it was getting dark. There was one instance when he was caught walking up the road as night approached. In the country, the darkness has a way of overcoming everything, making it difficult to see even a short distance ahead. The woods come alive with the most amazing sounds, leaving one to wonder if the animals nearby are merely warning their friends of your presence or if they are stalking you, waiting for their chance to attack.

On that occasion, Foggdog made it home safely but learned a valuable lesson. From then on, he always made sure to allow plenty of time to make it home while there was still daylight. Had he known the weather he would face this time, he surely would have given himself some extra time.

At first, it was merely a few innocent flurries – nothing we hadn't seen in recent weeks. For roughly an hour they fell, coating the ground with a thin film of white dust. Anna always loved playing in the snow, so we bundled up and went outdoors. As the accumulation slowly began to build, we were able to scrape some snow up off the ground and pack it into snowballs.

After all the work we had done to get the yard into shape for next year's planting, I couldn't remember the last time that I actually laughed and had fun. But when Anna snuck up on Mitch and nailed him in the neck with a cold, well-packed snowball, I was suddenly reminded. We all laughed heartily as a snowball fight erupted in the now expanded backyard of our beautiful country home. Sides were chosen, forts were built and snowballs were thrown from great distances, some hitting their target and some not. It was good to feel like a kid again. I had forgotten for so long what it was like to have pure, carefree fun.

We stayed outdoors for as long as we could before the wind suddenly picked up and the snow began to fall harder. It was starting to get dark out anyway, so we decided it was time to go inside.

Laughter still hung in the air as Charlotte began heating up some water on the stove to make us all a round of hot chocolate. Anna and I sat at the table doing our best impression of Mitch's reaction to being hit by the snowball.

"How about the part where the ice went down his shirt?" I asked.

Anna grabbed at her shirt-collar, faked a surprised look and then screamed with a little added femininity for effect. She then hopped around the room, continuing to mock Mitch, much to my enjoyment. Mitch, on the other hand, didn't appear to find it as funny. Instead of laughing along in self-deprecating fashion, he just stood at the back door, staring out the window towards the storm.

"Come on," I said. "Laugh a little."

The best I could get out of him was a bit of a smile, and then he turned back towards the window.

"It's getting really bad out there," he reported.

Looking outside, it was easy to confirm Mitch's observation. The snow was thick and the wind whipped it around in a blinding frenzy. Having been so captivated by the fun we were having, I had forgotten one other detail of which Mitch was about to remind me:

"...and Foggdog is still out there."

"Dammit," I cursed, my frustration turned inward for not remembering that my friend was out there braving the elements to get home.

I picked up my cell phone and called him, predictably getting no answer. Charlotte brought over a round of hot chocolates on a tray, but I was now too lost in worry to care for mine. Sensing my concern, she tried to reassure us that Foggdog would be safe.

"He left a long time ago. I'm sure he'll be here soon. He's a big, strong guy – he can walk through this."

"I don't know," Mitch said. "It's really bad out there and he should have been home by now. I'm going to go out and look for him."

Mitch picked up his coat and began to re-dress himself to go out into the cold.

I made eye contact with Charlotte and she nodded in approval before I even had to say it. "I'm going, too. There are only a couple of inches on the ground. We'll take the truck."

There was never a dull moment in this new world in which we lived. Just as I thought I might have found fun and laughter, the reality of the situation struck home and I was now headed out on a rescue mission in a blizzard.

"Just be careful," Charlotte said.

"I will."

My hat and coat were on in no time and I threw my gloves in my pocket. Opening the door, we were met with a freezing gust of wind that brought a burst of snow through the door before we walked out. Shielding our eyes, we made it to the garage where I pushed the button to open the automatic door and then hopped in the driver's seat.

Firing up the truck, I noted the gas gauge was pretty low. We tried not to drive too often, using fuel sparingly during our yard work, mostly to rip out tree stumps. There was maybe one more full, two-gallon container in the garage and the brownouts seemed to be occurring more frequent lately, causing us to fire up the generator more often than I had hoped.

Now the truck was nearly on empty and we had to trek out into the snow to find Foggdog. Mitch sensed my angst and looked at the needle himself.

"Should we put some more in the tank?" he asked.

"No," I responded. "We'll use what we've got. It'll keep us honest. We can't afford to drive around the neighborhood looking for Foggdog."

"Ray," he pleaded. "He's our friend. We have to do what we can to find him."

I kept the truck in park and threw both hands on the wheel in frustration, knowing he was right. If we drove down the hill and ran out of gas without finding him, I would never be able to forgive myself. Especially if the result wasn't pleasant, like Foggdog being lost, or us being caught down the hill in a snowstorm with no way to get back home to help Charlotte protect the house.

"Alright," I surrendered. "One more gallon."

Getting out of the truck, I retrieved the gas can and emptied half of it into the tank as it idled. Then I hopped back in and flicked the headlights on as I inched the car out of the garage.

"Holy shit," Mitch said.

The snow was blinding and I could barely see the road ahead. I flicked on the high-beams, but that just made it worse and I immediately shut them off opting for the regular headlights, as bad as they were. It was beginning to look like a lost cause – how would we be able to find Foggdog if we couldn't even see but a few feet ahead of the truck?

Inching forward slowly, we eventually reached the big oak tree, its leafless branches offering little relief from the whipping snow. I pressed on the gas a little harder, but just at that moment a figure appeared directly in front of the headlights. Raising its arms up as if to flag us down, we knew right away it was Foggdog.

I quickly jammed on the brakes trying to stop the truck, but it didn't respond. Rather, it entered a slow skid on the frozen, snowed-over road until it hit into the obstruction which just presented itself amidst the blinding snow. We weren't moving very fast and the thumping noise of steel-versus-man wasn't very loud, but certainly audible. It wasn't more that a second or two after impact that the truck found its traction and finally stopped.

Mitch and I leapt into the cold, vicious night as fast as we could, looking underneath for verification of what we already knew. Sure enough, Foggdog's body lay there beneath the truck.

"Jimmy," I called, opting for his real name. "Are you ok?"

I could see him rolling around a bit under there, and finally he rolled in my direction.

"Hell, yeah," he said over the roaring of the truck engine that was but a few feet from his head. "At least it's not snowing under here!"

Mitch helped Foggdog out from under the truck and we got him to his feet. He didn't seem injured, but he was a little worse for wear after his trek in the snow. Mitch helped him walk back to the house, while I slowly and skillfully returned the truck to its home in the garage.

The short walk between the garage and the house was a lot easier knowing that I wasn't going back outside again, especially since I was anxious to check on Foggdog's condition.

Walking in the door, I could see everyone seated together at the kitchen table. Foggdog had a blanket draped over his head and was sipping from a mug.

"Is that?" I began to ask.

"Your hot chocolate," Charlotte finished.

"Damn," I said, shooting her a look of death. I really wanted that hot chocolate.

"You have arms and legs," she said. "Go make another."

So I did… I poured the water in the pot and set it on the gas stove while Foggdog recovered from his winter adventure. Most notably, I could tell that Anna was happy to see her friend home safe. As he warmed up, he relived the tale of how he survived the walk up the hill in the blizzard-like conditions. To hear him tell it, you would think he was out there for a week braving bears, wolves and starvation, with the potential irony of his journey's culminating in being run over by his friend's truck as he tried to flag him down.

It seemed such a Foggdog-like thing to do – carelessly walking home, as it got dark into a snowstorm, causing us to go out to look for him, potentially wasting the last remnants of our gasoline. But even I couldn't blame him for this one. We had no idea how bad the snow was going to be – there was no warning. Of course, what we didn't know was that it had only just begun.

The water grew hot enough for me to pour a cup of hot chocolate and head over to the table. Finally, I could mentally return to where I was before and just enjoy a calm, silent moment. But as I sat down to join my family and friends, the lights began to flicker. For an instant, it felt as though it would be just a flicker and everything would be okay again, but a second or two later the worst was confirmed: the power went out.

What we didn't understand at that moment was that it would be a long, long time before it would ever return. Instead, we did what we would have done in any previous storm. We got the flashlights and lit candles around the house. Mitch grabbed some wood we had stacked on the porch and attempted to light a fire in the fireplace. We hoped that by stacking it on the porch the wood would stay dry.

But with the crazy wind out there, it didn't matter. It took a while, but eventually Mitch succeeded in getting the fire lit. Once it blazed for a while, it was just a matter of getting new logs on it before the old ones fizzled out.

"The generator?" Charlotte asked me.

The thought of going out to the garage and wheeling over the generator in the blizzard was not a pleasant one. Having just seen how little gas we had left, and knowing that this blackout was not one of our normal brownouts but the result of what was becoming a pretty nasty storm, it was time for me to make a decision.

"I think we're going to leave the generator in the garage this time."

"But the freezer," Charlotte protested. "Isn't everything going to go bad?"

Looking at Mitch and then at Foggdog, it was clear they shared similar concerns.

"There's not much left anyway," I explained. "We can leave the rest in the freezer overnight and then eat some in the morning. Maybe if there's snow on the ground, we can cook everything and then put it in the snow for as long as it will keep. Once the roads clear up, Foggdog can take some of the leftover meat down to the Marino's."

They didn't seem happy with this answer.

"Look, we hardly have any gas left in the garage and we may really need it at some point. This is not just a normal brownout – this is a blackout from the storm. Maybe a tree fell on a power line or something and if that's the case, who knows how long the power will be out?"

This was indeed a concern. Nobody knew who worked for the power companies anymore or how to even get in touch with them. I hadn't seen a bill in months, but the electric kept pumping. Outside of the brownouts, we were beginning to take it for granted that we would just always have electricity. What we didn't know then was that our beautiful house on the hill wouldn't see a watt of it for years after that day.

"He's right," Mitch conceded. "There's not much gasoline left out there. It would probably run the generator for a day or two, but if the power doesn't come back then we'll have all but wasted it."

Once we had done all we could do, we sat in the living room

looking at one another. There was a radio and plenty of batteries, but all the local radio stations had gone out of business. There wasn't much on the radio out here in the country anyway, but all we could get on this night was static. Television, of course, was gone.

We began to mill about the house, but always returned to the warm comfort of the fireplace. On one occasion, Anna brought in my old acoustic guitar from the basement.

"Does this still work, Daddy?"

I hadn't played in years, but it was sort-of like riding a bike. "Let's see," I said, as I took the guitar from her and began tuning the strings.

"What are you doing, Dad?"

"I'm trying to tune the strings, Anna. The sound from each string has to mesh with each other in order for it to sound right."

It took me a while to remember the proper way to tune it, but all we had was time at this point. It was dark outside and the snow was still coming down. It had been about two hours since I had nearly killed one of my best friends with my truck, but there was at least a foot of snow out there already and the breeze was causing it to drift in spots, making it even worse. Every once in a while, we'd hear a large cracking noise outside – the result of a tree branch succumbing to the weight of the snow combined with the force of the wind.

Finally, I had the guitar tuned to the point it seemed playable. I rang out a few chords, and though I could tell it wasn't perfect, it seemed good enough for now.

"Play a song, Daddy."

I knew that was going to be the inevitable request, and there were only a handful of songs I thought I might remember. One came to mind right away, if only the first few lines:

"She's a good girl, loves her mama…"

Tom Petty's *Free Fallin'* was just an introduction and I wound up playing just about everything I could remember that night. I made a mental note to look for guitar tablature for other songs the next time we visited the library.

Without electricity, without light, we wound up having a very enjoyable evening. I carried Anna up to bed, noticing the house was getting very cold. Not only was the electricity gone, but it seemed as though so was the heat. This would be the last night we would all sleep up in the bedrooms. I knew that the water pump for the well wouldn't be working the next day either, and after the water in the tank was used up, we'd have to figure something else out. I put it out of my mind for the moment.

We said good night and Mitch took his place at the window taking the first watch.

"You gonna be able to wake up with no alarm tonight?" he asked me. I had batteries in the basement that would run my alarm clock, but I figured I had an easier way.

"I'll use my phone alarm," I said, holding it up and turning it on. I found myself staring down at the photo I had taken of Anna outside the library with the rainbow streaking across the sky behind her. It was taken just a few months back, but already she looked different to me. I knew that these times could have aged anyone and perhaps my eyes were merely jaded from my experience. But I wished like hell that every day could be like that day.

Mitch noticed I was taking a while, but allowed me my moment. I finally decided it was time to set the alarm, but just as I went to do so I noticed one more problem: the phone's battery was dying.

"Oh, shit," I said.

"What?" asked Mitch.

The screen went dark.

"Fuck!"

"What?"

"The battery died."

"No big deal," Mitch said. "I'll come wake you up."

"No, it's not that," I said. My concern wasn't that I would miss my wake up call. My concern was that with no electricity, I had no idea when the next time I would be able to see the pictures and videos I had taken over the years. In particular, I wondered if I would ever see that picture of my daughter in the last perfect moment I could remember before everything changed.

THE ENDING

CHAPTER FOURTEEN

Mitch and I walked out of the woods carrying the shovels we had just used to dig the final resting place of my friend, Art Brady. It was a lonely way to say goodbye to a man who was so popular among the townspeople, but there was nothing else we could really do. We didn't want it known that Art had snuck out of the camp and got his message to us.

The woods were still wet with the rains from the past few days – the leaves were still moist and the ground muddy. It was warm, and the smell of spring hung in the air – the first time I had sensed it this year. Usually, this would bring great joy as a sign that we were ushering in the good weather and saying good-bye to the winter. Despite the sullen mood given the task we had just performed, it felt natural to be encouraged by that familiar smell - only this year, spring was bringing on nothing but hard work and pressure to generate a crop that would feed our family for an extended period of time. It felt wrong not to enjoy the first sign of spring, but under the circumstances it was nearly impossible.

Digging a six foot ditch to bury a body was something I never thought I would have to do. It had taken up a fair amount of the morning and by the time Mitch and I got back to the house, the girls were still there but Foggdog had gone. This was a big dereliction of duty in the house as we never left the ladies at home alone.

"He's where?" I asked Charlotte with an edge of anger she certainly detected.

"Where do you think? He went to see Katie."

Mitch and I made eye contact and both rolled our eyes.

"Oh, take it easy on him," Charlotte said. "He hasn't seen her in three days. The boy is in love."

"That boy has never been in love," I observed.

"Well maybe he's turned over a new leaf. Besides, he left me the gun and I'm not completely defenseless you know. I can handle myself."

Charlotte removed the pistol from her apron and handed it back to Mitch. Mitch was the only one licensed to carry it, but in this world I'm not so sure that licenses mattered much anymore. I noted a change in her attitude that day. A few months ago she seemed nervous about the possibility of intruders and random vagabonds, but now she seemed hardened and tough. I wasn't sure if that was a good thing, but I was happy she didn't seem afraid anymore.

"Charlotte and Anna are home alone, Foggdog is wandering down the hill all by himself, we're walking through the woods with a dead body and we only have one gun to protect us all," I said. It seemed like things were getting way too weird and we were beginning to lose our discipline. So, I recommended doing the only thing I could think to do. "Maybe it's time to go through those cards and see if we can salvage some information."

"I'm going outside to get some work done," Mitch said. "It's almost planting season and we have to be ready."

"Ok," I said.

With that, Mitch headed outdoors, Charlotte headed back to Anna's playroom to work on her schooling and I went to the office to see what kind of information I could glean from a stack of wet, splotchy index cards.

I pulled open the shades to allow as much of the natural light to come in as possible. At this hour the sun normally shined brightly through the window, but it was still a little overcast from all the rain and the room remained mostly dim. The stack of cards in front of me looked like a hopeless task. They were still mostly damp and the edges of each card were welded to one another, essentially creating one large, paper brick. I opened the drawer and took out anything that looked like a tool I might be able to use – paperclips, pens, a staple remover, and a letter opener.

The top card was completely illegible. The ink had run and it was just a big, blotchy, blue stain across the front. I hoped to find better luck underneath. Trying the letter opener first, I attempted to glide it underneath the first card, but with no luck. I was only ripping the cards further.

Unwinding a paperclip, I thought it might be better if I tried again with a smaller tool. The cards still ripped, but not as much as they had with the letter opener. I decided to keep going, and after some time I had traced the entire outer edge of the top card, though it was still stuck to the one underneath. Now that the edges were traced around, I tried with the letter opener again, slowly and smoothly sliding it between the top card and the one underneath.

When it finally made it to the other end, I held my breath and closed my eyes hoping that I hadn't done more harm than good with my surgical skills. Lifting the top card, the one underneath was revealed and I opened my eyes.

"Much better," I whispered to myself. The second card wasn't perfect, but it was better than the top one. I could make out most of a name and an address. There was a list of arms – a couple of rifles and boxes of ammunition located in the basement. "No Alarm – just break a window, I won't mind," it instructed.

I put the card aside and started on the next level of the stack, and then the next, and the next. The process was tedious, but the information seemed too important not to continue on. Searching the drawers of the desk, I found a street map I had bought when we moved in. Removing some pictures from the far wall, I pinned the map up despite knowing that Charlotte would disapprove of this new decorating scheme. I then placed pins at the locations of houses listed on the cards, while also keeping a chart on a legal pad of the names, addresses and what we could expect to find there.

As I delved through the stack of cards, each new one proved clearer than the last. Some of the ones in the middle were nearly pristine and I could easily take down all of the information.

Two hours passed and I was on a roll, flying through the cards, categorizing the information and marking up the map. Mitch peeked in at one point and was startled at the size of the operation I had begun.

"Can I help?" he asked.

"Of course. I probably should try to make sense of what it is that I'm doing here anyway."

He sat down and I showed him the information I had found. I

recognized some of the names on the cards and was shocked at some of the items listed. A sniper rifle, pistols, shotguns, ammunition and one card listed "live grenades," and in parenthesis "Don't ask, just take them."

In all, there were about 50 cards and I had gotten through all of them but the last few. Most of the cards were completely legible, a few completely wasted and some cards could be partially read and frustratingly incomplete. On the whole, Art had done a great job keeping them dry given the circumstances.

Mitch helped me finish the last few and when we were done, we had a map with randomly pinned locations and a list of local weapons caches waiting for us to collect. I leaned back and sighed.

"What are you thinking?" Mitch asked.

"I don't know," I said, perfectly aware of the conundrum lying ahead of us.

"I think I know what you're thinking," he observed.

I explained. "These people went through the trouble of secretly writing down this information, sending a courier through the rain on a desperate mission to help liberate them. That mission would take the courier's life. He also happened to be a friend of mine. The question is, do we go ahead and plan some sort of attack on the camp, or do we selfishly take all these weapons for our own personal defense?"

"That seems to sum it up," he said.

Charlotte entered the room and we immediately ceased all discussion. She most certainly would have detected the awkwardness had there not been something there to distract her. Looking at the office wall, she shook her head at the large map that now hung there. "Oh my," she said.

"I guess I got a little carried away," I admitted.

"No... no, this is amazing," she said walking over to it. "We probably have more information on our neighbors than the CIA." She ran her fingers over the pins on the map, starting at the ones closest to our house trying to figure out if I had marked off anyone she knew. "Is this...???" she pointed.

"Mrs. Quigley's house, yes," I answered. "Apparently Mrs. Quigley has a strong belief in the second amendment."

We all sat staring for a moment, remembering what Art had told us in his last moments about the suffering of our friends.

"What are we going to do?" she asked calmly, placing the discussion exactly where we had left it before she entered.

Nobody had an answer.

"This is not our war," I started. "As much as I feel for our neighbors and their situation, this was their decision. We decided to go it alone, to avoid the camps, and we have enough responsibilities here as it is without the risk of a life-threatening military assault on a government installation."

"Gee, when you put it that way," Mitch said, nodding in agreement.

"But they're our neighbors," Charlotte protested. "Maybe we can pass the message on to someone who might do something."

"Absolutely not," I said. "If we get implicated in planning an attack or if they figure out that Art made his way up here, we'll be in just as much trouble as if we stormed the camps holding guns."

That answer seemed to sit well with Mitch, but surprisingly not as much with Charlotte, who looked angry at my resistance.

"And what would happen if I was killed?" I asked. "What would you and Anna do up here?"

"We'd still have Foggdog," she said, drawing a light-hearted chuckle from us both. The laugh cut the tension and relaxed the room.

"Maybe this isn't something we can just decide all at once," I commented.

"True," Mitch agreed. "Why do we have to decide right at this moment?"

"So," I continued. "Let's do this. Let's gather as much of the weaponry as we can and build up the supply. We need weapons for ourselves anyway – pistols for each of us when we split up and rifles for hunting. Maybe by the time we collect them all, we'll have a better sense of what we should do."

Mitch and Charlotte nodded in agreement. Frankly, I didn't think there was any other choice in the matter.

"First things first, though," I said. "We can't forget our responsibilities here. It's spring and tomorrow, we begin planting. When we get time, we'll begin collecting the weapons. "

Making sure we had enough to eat was still our highest priority. We would have plenty of time afterwards to collect the weapons and figure out whether or not we should plan an assault against the government-run labor camp and free the prisoners.

CHAPTER FIFTEEN

The next morning we went straight to work. Even Foggdog woke up early, knowing if he missed helping out on planting day he would be in serious trouble. As we planted the seeds for what we hoped would be a bountiful food supply, we filled him in on the information we had found and the plan at hand.

The day went on and the work kept our minds occupied. We planted a number of different crops – tomatoes, cucumbers, peppers, zucchini, squash, lettuce, eggplant, broccoli, cauliflower – all in hopes that we could grow enough food that, combined with our improving hunting and trapping skills, would keep us fed through the next year.

Anna loved the day outdoors and helped us plant our crops. She worked just as hard as everyone else, but as the day went on and we lost steam, she began to bound about the field with the eternal energy of a child. It was nice to be able to inject an ounce of fun into what otherwise was a day of hard work and sweat. It made an otherwise difficult task somewhat bearable.

It was late afternoon when Foggdog announced that he was ready to head back down to Katie's house for the night.

"You know, we need you to keep watch up here," I said. I was getting a little sick of his absences when we were at a loss for manpower at the house.

"I know, I know," he explained. "But I have to go see her; I told her I would go back tonight."

He had never gone down there for the whole night before and it was always implied that he was needed to help us keep watch.

Otherwise, the rest of us would have to be up longer to cover his shift. Even though we were all in pretty good shape after months of clearing the field, everyone needed sleep to rest up for the working days ahead.

I sighed and glanced at Charlotte who was giving me a look as if to say "cut him a break." In fairness, he had worked a very hard day and I almost felt as though he had earned it. But with one gun and only two of us taking shifts, this was starting to feel a little dangerous. "Ok, on one condition," I said, knowing that I really didn't have any negotiating leverage other than Foggdog's personal guilt towards leaving us for the night.

"Name it," he said.

"On the condition that before you go, we head to the nearest location on that map – the McCulloughs. Supposedly we will find a rifle in the basement, and a handgun and ammo in an upstairs safe. You can take the handgun," I said to him, "to keep you safe on the road. We can start using the rifle for hunting."

"Deal," Foggdog said. "Let's go."

I went into the office and retrieved my notes on the McCullough residence, which was less than a half-mile down the road. Even though it was low on gas, the three of us jumped in the truck, which we decided to use since it was our first pick-up and we wanted it to go as smoothly as possible. We were all a little nervous and it didn't help that we had left Charlotte and Anna at home alone and unarmed, but we wanted this to be quick.

Pulling up to the house, we were glad to see the place was quiet, with no signs of any recent human presence. The house was two floors, of which the top one had two single windows to the right, and a large bay window to the left. I guessed that the bay window probably was in the living room and the single windows were probably the bedrooms. Quickly walking to the front of the house, I smashed a window as the card had instructed and before we knew it, we were inside.

From there, we split up. I headed down to the basement to look for the rifle, while Mitch and Foggdog headed upstairs to locate the safe. The basement storage area was an impossible mess to navigate, especially in the dark, and it took me a while to wade through the boxes before finding the rifle hung up on a wall. I carefully removed it from its rack before looking around for any boxes of shells or ammo I might find, with no luck.

Foggdog and Mitch were back within minutes and our plan was to be in-and-out as quickly as possible, no matter the desire to check things out. After all, this was somebody else's home.

"I have the rifle," I said, "but no ammunition."

"That's okay," Mitch answered. "We found the handgun in the safe with boxes of ammunition for both the handgun and the rifle."

"Good."

"We should look around a bit," Foggdog added. "There's got to be things we can use."

"No," I said. "That's not what we're here for. These people gave us their trust when they wrote their info on the card and I will not betray that. We are not thieves."

"Not even this?" Foggdog asked, holding up a Costco-sized package of toilet paper. If there was one supply which was becoming dangerously low, that was it. I succumbed to the temptation.

"Okay, but only that."

And then we left.

We made it home that evening with a feeling of exhilaration and two new firearms. Foggdog took the new handgun with him on his way to Katie's, and we now had Mitch's gun and a rifle as well. I slept like a baby that night, at least when it wasn't my watch.

Over the next few days we spent time alternating between working in the fields and collecting weapons (and toilet paper) from the houses on the list. We always took great care to stay only as long as needed.

After hitting up the McCulloughs' place on that first day, we couldn't afford to use the truck anymore. There was just not enough gas. But we felt a little safer riding the bikes now that we were each armed. It was also less nerve-wracking knowing that Charlotte was armed in the home while we left.

As time went by, we were more than halfway through the cards and the basement was beginning to resemble an armory. Though part of me abhorred the thought of keeping weapons downstairs in the house when I could keep them in the garage instead, it seemed more important to keep them under lock and key, literally under our own feet, than to risk them being stolen by a stealthy thief in the night.

Next on our list were a string of three houses next to each other about ten miles away from our home. The trip was a little more involved than usual. A 10-mile ride wasn't a big deal for the three of us, but the bounty would be a bit more than we were used to carrying. The third house on the list was the one with the live grenades. "Don't ask... just take them," the note said. The ride there would be a breeze, but ten miles back with backpacks full of guns, ammunition, and live grenades was another story.

We were in and out of the first two houses quickly after finding a couple of rifles and a pretty high-powered handgun with lots of ammo. We were all looking forward to the third house – the one with the grenades.

We approached the house the same way we did the dozens of homes before it, with caution and a sense of expediency. Walking toward the garage, I read the paper one last time – there were two sets of instructions. One was a code to get into the garage and the other said, "If there is no electricity, then run a credit card through the door latch leading to the garage. Do the same for the door leading to the basement from the garage and walk up the basement stairs to the house."

The instructions were fairly specific. The homeowner had clearly thought about whether there was electricity or not and nobody else had thought about this important detail. Like all the other houses we had visited, there were no lights on and a general sense of abandonment. We parked the bikes behind a bush on the front lawn, leaving behind a backpack we had filled from the first two houses.

I tried the garage code first but, as expected, it didn't respond. We finagled the lock and made our way inside the garage. The inside door that led to the basement was just as easy to open and we headed down the stairs.

Everything had always gone so smoothly according to the instructions on the cards. We breached every home quickly, quietly and without incident. We retrieved every weapon just as if it had been placed there perfectly for us to take.

Perhaps we had gotten a little too complacent.

As we ascended the stairs to the home, the door ahead of us quickly opened and we heard the familiar clicking sound of a pump-action rifle as a man entered the stairwell and pointed the gun in our direction.

In the past, we might have had our guns drawn, but after some time we realized that these houses were all abandoned and we felt as though there was more danger in having guns drawn than not. With the three of us sneaking around a dimly-lit, unknown house, we didn't want one of us to accidentally shoot the other. We carried the guns, but never had them drawn. Of course, with the barrel of a shotgun leveled at us, it seemed a little too late to adjust that policy.

Instinctively, our hands immediately hit the air. We weren't ready to fight. At this point, we were only hoping the man in front of us wouldn't kill us.

"Who the fuck are you and what are you doing here?" he demanded.

"I can explain, I can explain," I said.

"You better explain," the man said as he pointed the rifle directly in my face.

Remembering the name on the card, thankful that it was one of the more pristine cards in the stack, I answered, "Chuck Rose sent me."

There was a brief moment of silence as it seemed as though something had registered in our captor's mind. I was hoping it was something positive.

"How do you know Chuck?" he asked.

I contemplated lying and saying that Chuck and I were long-time friends and that he sent us there to check on his home. But I truly didn't know anything else about this man other than how to break into his home and what was in it. So I chose another path... I chose the truth.

"I don't. Actually, I don't know him at all." I could sense Foggdog sighing behind me as if he were disapproving of my honesty.

I could see the man's grip tightening on the shotgun and thought I might be in some serious trouble. But I tried not to show fear or weakness, rather a firm sense that we belonged there. He eventually broke.

"Up here. All of you, upstairs." We followed his instructions at gunpoint and found ourselves in the middle of the kitchen. "Against the wall." We complied.

"Any of you assholes armed?"

"All of us are," I admitted. "We'll be happy to disarm if you like." I was just trying to stay in control and keep things calm. I wasn't concerned with Mitch – he was solid. But Foggdog could crack at any point. I knew that by keeping my wits about me, it would allow him to feel more at ease with the situation.

"Tell me where they are and I'll get them," he said.

One by one the man went down the line and took our guns from us. Now we were completely helpless and for the first time I thought about Charlotte and Anna, and what would happen to them if we didn't wind up coming home tonight.

Although concerning, the thought of it was also distracting and I tried my best to put it out of my mind.

"Sit down at the table and keep your hands where I can see 'em," he said. We did, placing our hands flat on the circular kitchen table.

"How do you know Chuck?" he asked again.

"I told you," I tried to explain calmly, "I don't. I am here because Chuck sent me a note so that I could retrieve some items from the house for him."

"Bullshit," he said. "Chuck would never let someone into his house. Why the hell would he do that?"

"I can explain," I said. "But it's a long story."

"We have all the time in the world."

So I began to tell him the story, starting with how we had decided to go it alone instead of going to the food camps, followed by the visit we got from Art.

It was then that I realized this was going to be a turning point in our thought process. Right at this moment, I was crossing a line. We had collected a number of weapons – nearly completing the whole stack of Art's cards. All along I was hoping there would be a way to get around actually planning an armed assault on the camp. But this was the only legitimate reason for me to be in a house ten miles from home to retrieve weapons. To say I was getting the weapons to protect my own family was to say I was stealing them for my own selfish use. And the only way to appease the man in the room holding a gun was to get him to believe that I was going to liberate the camps. In essence, I needed to recruit him to our side.

So I did my best. The longer I spoke, the longer the man with the gun seemed to accept our company and the more I convinced myself that the right thing to do was to liberate the camp, even though I wasn't really sure how that might get done.

I finished the story and the room grew silent. "I have the card your uncle sent me in a backpack outside, if you want to see it."

"No," he said. "I believe you. You have his name, you have his address, and you knew the exact location of where he stashed his weapons. I think you're telling the truth. Besides, I'm not really supposed to be here myself. I just didn't have any place to go." He lowered the gun. "This is my uncle's house. He was always a fighter... a survivor. I was shocked that he wasn't here when I arrived last week. I'm even more shocked that he went to some government camp."

"People were surprised by this thing," I offered. "They thought the camps were innocent and temporary. Nobody thought it would turn out like this."

We sat for a moment as our captor pondered the information he had just been given. He seemed to be at ease.

"We cool?" I asked.

"Yeah," he said. "Yeah, we're cool."

And with that, he lowered the gun and we all took a sigh of relief. "My name's Colin. Colin Rose," he said. "And I'm in. I'm with you."

CHAPTER SIXTEEN

I kept my watch that night as a light, foggy mist fell out the window, making it somewhat difficult to see. The cold winter had mostly subsided, giving way to the wetness of a typical New England spring. We probably could have re-occupied the bedrooms during our regular sleeping hours, but we had grown used to the living room and it still tended to get cold at night. So we kept the mattresses on the floor and the fireplace lit; at least, for now.

The night was quiet and began to give way to morning. I had slept for a few hours before my watch and I was feeling pretty energetic. Keeping watch at night was always a necessary, yet monotonous task that usually resulted in nothing but providing time for me to sit and think. Tonight I tried to regroup and think about how I was going to deal with the past day's occurrences.

As much as I was happy that Colin Rose had the good sense not to shoot us, I was a little concerned over his zealousness to join the cause. Up until that point, "the cause" was just that – a cause and not much more. Now we had used it to negotiate our escape, and a week from now Colin would be coming by the house expecting a work-in-progress. All we had was a thumbtacked-map and a basement of arms.

When I thought about our role in a potential liberation scenario, everything always came back to Anna. Certainly, her potential to thrive in life would be much better if her father was alive. At least, *I* thought so. Yet on the other hand, what would she think about her dad years from now if he had done nothing and allowed our friends and neighbors to live under conditions we never thought could exist in this country?

There was certainly danger in living at the house and who knows how long we would remain safe up here. The world outside seemed a lot more like the Wild, Wild West. I wasn't ready to fully commit myself to planning this assault, but my firm foundation against it had certainly weakened.

The fields were planted and the rain meant we would not have to water at all today. In fact, we had done so much work out there that we were due for a day off. Charlotte awoke at daylight, as she usually did. Often times she would take over for me at this time and spend the next few hours on watch before we all got up for the day.

"Do you want to get some sleep?" she asked.

"No. I have a lot to do today. I can't afford to sleep."

She put her arms around my neck and gave me a toothpaste-flavored kiss. "You know it turns me on when you talk like that," she admitted.

We held each other tightly for a few moments longer than a normal, everyday hug. It was an embrace that gave us confidence that we were supportive of our decisions so far, and we were very much teammates in this going forward. Her support meant everything to me. I couldn't go forward without it, and after a night of deep introspection and thought, this moment provided me all the support I needed.

The regular waking pattern followed, with Anna and Mitch rising at about the same time and Foggdog lazily sleeping the morning away. I swear he'd sleep all day if we let him, but I wasn't going to let him. Not today.

"Get up, lazy ass," I barked.

He wrestled around his chair, stretching and appearing agitated.

"C'mon, we've gotta go."

"What? What?" he began. "Where? Where we goin'?"

"To visit your girlfriend."

For a brief moment, he looked confused before realizing I was dead serious. So, he got up and began to change into clean clothes.

"Can I shower first?" he asked.

"Five minutes," I demanded. Showers usually took much longer these days as we had to drag water from the nearby pond and boil it. We kept a pretty hefty supply of it in the house and showers weren't really showers, but more like sponge-baths. However, saying "I'm going to shower," still felt normal and some things we didn't want to change.

It took him more like ten minutes, but I was happy enough that he was awake and moving that I didn't bother him about it. I kissed Anna and Charlotte good-bye before we jumped on the bikes and headed down the hill.

"Can I just ask a question?" Foggdog inquired.

"You just did."

"Why do *you* want to see *my* girlfriend?"

It was just like him to ask such a stupid question. He always had trouble seeing the big picture.

"I don't want to see Katie, you fool," I said, shaking my head. "I need to speak with her father and her brothers."

That seemed to click with him, and he was mostly silent the rest of the ride. I knew Katie's father somewhat, which is to say that I knew who he was. We had met a few times, but I couldn't say I knew him all that well. After the winter storm, we had sent down some of the extra meat we had been keeping in the snow. It would have gone bad had we left it out there much longer and there was too much of it for us to eat. The Marinos were thankful, and began sending Foggdog home with eggs from their chickens. So, even though I hadn't met the man, we were at least aware of each other and seemingly on good terms.

Ed Marino had a tough exterior and seemed very gruff and unapproachable. I wasn't surprised to hear that he and his family, which consisted of three boys and their younger sister, decided to stay home and rough it rather than go to the food camps. I also had no idea how he allowed his youngest daughter to date a guy like Foggdog, but somehow they got along. Foggdog must have turned on the charm for the old man just as hard as he had for his daughter.

The Marinos had a farm much bigger than the one in our backyard and they had the manpower and the experience to run it. Other than the crops, they also raised chickens and pigs.

Once we lost the freezer from the power outage, we were left with only dried and canned foods. Our hunting and trapping skills were not very successful outside of a few rabbits and a wild turkey. We had largely become vegetarians, though not necessarily by choice. I never thought I'd feel so grateful just to see some plain old eggs. It almost made up for Foggdog's absence from work duty around the house.

I had only sent notice of our gratitude through word-of-mouth, so I figured it was about time I extended that gratitude personally and perhaps slipped in a word or two about our potential plans to liberate Maly Farms. I could tell Foggdog was a little nervous as we pulled the bikes into the driveway. What a strange feeling this must be for him: a 35-year old man riding a bicycle to his girlfriend's house. But this was the world we lived in.

He rang the bell and after a few moments Katie answered, looking happily surprised to see him at this early hour. After embracing him, she turned and seemed a bit shocked to see me standing there.

"Mr. Stanton," she said, "What are you doing here?"

"Hey Katie," I said. "I figured I'd stop by finally to thank your Dad and your brothers for all the eggs you guys have been sending our way."

"You didn't have to do that. It's a long ride down here and Jimmy has been plenty thankful on your behalf. Especially after the basket we sent up last week."

I smirked at Foggdog, who had a guilty look on his face. There was no basket of eggs two weeks ago – he had apparently eaten them all. I seethed at the thought he would keep food from us after all of our hospitality – especially from Anna. But there was no time to be angry; there was a bigger mission ahead of me.

We walked into the house and Katie led us out back where her three brothers were already working away in the fields and Ed Marino was out by the chicken coop. He noticed us immediately and walked over.

"Good morning, Ed," I offered, shaking his hand.

"Good morning, Ray" he reciprocated. "Mornin', Jimmy," he greeted Foggdog with a nod. "What brings you out here this fine morning? Surely, you all got work to do getting ready for the season?" He spoke with a sort-of slight southern drawl that was actually fairly common amongst some rural Northerners.

"Well, I wanted to thank you for the batches of eggs you've been sending home with Fogg…,"I caught myself before using the nickname that had become all too familiar with us. "…with Jimmy here. It's been a pretty hard winter, especially since the power went out."

"You're mighty welcome. We've had a lot of extra this year now that most of our friends have gone to the camps. To tell you the truth, I never once thought I'd be counting on those chickens for survival, but it seems to be a whole new world than what we've been used to."

"You're telling me."

"Can I get you a glass of water or something?" he asked hospitably. "Sorry I don't have much of a beverage selection. Actually, hold on a minute," Ed said, looking as though he'd just had a bright idea. "I'll be right back."

He got up and went back into the house. Foggdog and Katie held hands and followed, though I had a feeling they were off to someplace else. I stood out back and looked out over the fields. The men out there working were all probably right around my age, and all had come back home to work the family land once times started getting rough.

One of them took a moment out of his chores to look up and offer me a friendly wave, which I gladly returned. I had no idea which one was which – I didn't even really know their names. Even if I did, they all seemed to look alike from this distance. I couldn't help but think that these tall, strong, hard-working country boys would probably make excellent soldiers.

"Here ya' go," said Ed as he walked out the door offering me a can of beer.

"You've gotta be kidding me," I said. "I haven't seen one of these in months." It was still pretty early in the morning, but neither of us seemed to mind. I cracked it open and we gave a simultaneous, "Cheers!" before clicking the cans together and taking a sip.

"Yeah, we have a stash in the corner of the basement with some bottles of wine, trying to keep them cool. Supply is starting to run low, but you can't save 'em forever or they just don't taste right."

We sat at the table and sipped at the beer. It wasn't ice cold, but it didn't really matter. I was very happy I decided to take the trip down the hill today, but I was careful not to let Ed's generosity turn me into a softy.

"If you ever need some of those eggs," he said, "you just have Jimmy ask and we'll send a batch up. It's nice to know there are still good, honest people around these parts. We've had a lot of bandits and thieves comin' through here. It's just amazing what people will

119

resort to when they're in trouble. They don't work for themselves, but they don't mind taking from others to survive."

I often wondered if thievery was still prevalent around these parts, but once the television reports went off there was just no way to get any news. The Marinos lived much closer to the main part of town and if people were coming through, be it walking, riding a bike, or driving, they were much more likely to pass by the Marinos than to wander up our 2-mile hill. We had had the one incident months ago and then there was Art's visit, but other than that we had seen nobody up at the house.

"Have you had many problems here?" I asked.

"A few," he admitted. "See that bell over there?" he asked while pointing across the deck. I nodded. "If I ring that bell, those boys out there drop everything they got and come running this way. I go down to the basement and grab the shotguns. Most of the time when they see the four of us at the ready, they just move right on by."

The thought of Ed and his three boys standing in front of their home with guns certainly seemed intimidating enough to me.

"That bell has rung eight times over the past six months," he added.

"And…"

"And we're all still alive and nothing's been taken from us."

"Does Jimmy help out at all?" I asked.

"Heh," Ed chortled. "He was here one time. The boys and I scared away one bandit who wandered a little too close to the house. He was probably just looking to steal some food or somethin' – he didn't seem like much trouble. Jimmy stayed inside the whole time. Well, me and the boys gave him some shit for it. Now he knows the rules and I expect next time he's here and that bell rings, he'll be the first one standing next to me."

That sounded a lot like the Foggdog I knew.

"In the beginning things were a little more crazy," Ed continued. "A lot of people on the road – motorcycles, trucks, cars racing by. I'm sure lotsa people been robbed, but we've been able to scare 'em off every time. There aren't many people comin' around anymore. Seen some people on foot and even some people on horses a few days ago. I think everyone just ran out of gas."

That was certainly understandable. My own truck had just a small amount of gas left in it with an additional small amount in storage, and there was no telling how long that would last.

I was impressed with the Marinos' preparedness and it reminded me of the night that Art made his way to our house. We had no real plan for what to do next once we realized that a man was coming towards the house. But Ed had the whole plan – the bell, the guns, and a place to meet. This was the kind of guy I wanted on my side, and with that I began my pitch.

"Ed, there's another reason I came down here today – something else I wanted to talk to you about."

He perked up in his chair as if expecting a sales pitch, though he simply asked, "What's that?"

Suddenly I found myself a little nervous. The speech was so easy the day before when we sat at Colin's table with a gun to our heads. Of course, the cost of failure was a little higher then. Really, the cost of failure here was just as high. If Art was telling the truth, who knew how many people would eventually die in the labor camps before we could finally figure out a way to help them?

At risk now was the potential addition of four tough-minded, burly men who were well armed and intense. Their participation would double our current standing army. Truthfully, I had no real plan of action beyond recruiting the Marino family and now I felt the pressure of possible failure. If Colin showed up at the house next week and I had no other help, my credibility with him would be shot.

"Did you know Art Brady?" I began.

"Ol' Art from the gas station?" he asked. "Why sure."

I knew that Ed would know Art. Everyone knew Art.

"So you know that he went to the food camps, then."

"Well, I hadn't seen him around so I sort of guessed that was the case. It seems like most people around here reported to the camps."

"Yeah," I agreed. "It sure does. That whole 'mortgage-forgiveness' thing went a long way." The image of Art showing up at my doorstep immediately came to mind. And over the next few minutes, I tried to explain to Ed, in vivid detail, exactly how that night had gone. I conveyed everything from seeing Art come up the walk, to listening to him tell the story about how the promise of the food camps had developed into the horrid labor camps. I told him about the wet stack of cards we had deciphered and how we snuck around town retrieving weapons from random houses.

Ed's eyes seemed to widen as my story progressed, especially as I told him about how we went to retrieve the grenades and ran into the barrel-end of a shotgun.

"So we sat there at the table with a gun pointed at us, and I told the guy exactly what I've just told you."

"And he let you go?" Ed asked.

"No," I said. "He joined our cause."

Ed let out an audible sigh of relief. "So wait," he noted, finally realizing what it was that I was asking him. "Are you asking me to join you in an assault on the camp?"

"I'm telling you that I am contemplating planning an assault on the camp. Our friends and neighbors are being held there and are going through very tough times. They need help and I can't just stand by and do nothing. Now, our odds would certainly be better if we had you and your boys with us." With that, I sat forward in the chair and stared Ed right in the eyes to show him that I was deadly serious.

After a few seconds, Ed breathed out and sat back in his chair, his eyes diverting to his boys in the fields. "…and your wife?" he asked.

"She knows the importance of this," I explained. "She was right next to Art as he told his story and it affected her just like it affected me… as it is affecting you right now. This is not something we are taking lightly."

Ed stood up from his chair and sauntered over to the edge of the deck near the bell. He grabbed the rope and rung it 3 times.

At the onset of the first ring, the men in the fields dropped their tools and began running towards the house as if they were trained dogs. But once they looked up and heard the bell stop ringing, which must be the signal that it wasn't an emergency, the boys slowed to a walking pace and walked their way back to the house. Getting up from my chair, I walked over to greet them.

Ed let go of the rope and turned around. "Stopping the bell after three rings mean it's not an emergency, but they should come in anyway," he confirmed.

I stood next to Ed as we watched his sons make their way down the long, lined fields. It was perhaps the warmest day of the year so far, and the sun shone brightly through a mostly blue sky dotted with clouds. I couldn't help but think about how maybe in prior years, this might be the day that pools were opened, or barbeques lit.

As we waited for the boys to make their way in, suddenly the door to the house flew open, and a 200-pound whirlwind escaped the house as if it were on fire.

Foggdog.

"Where are they? Where are they? Can I have a gun?"

I looked at Ed and we couldn't help but burst out laughing. It had been so long since I laughed that my gut exploded in pain as though I had been stabbed. I grabbed at it, but it didn't help because I just could not stop laughing.

"What?" Foggdog asked. "What?"

The men were just getting back from the fields and could sense what had just happened and began chuckling themselves.

"Go get 'em, Jimmy!" one of them heckled, as Foggdog realized the joke was on him. He had no idea that three bells meant there was no emergency and was so earnest to prove his mettle after last time; his exuberance was reason for all of us to engage in a fit of laughter.

Katie followed outside to the deck, her shirt untucked and her hair a little messier than I remembered it from earlier. I looked at Foggdog, also noticing a bright pink, silkish-cloth protruding from the pocket in his pullover sweatshirt – Katie's bra!

He made eye-contact with me and though I was still laughing, I stared at the suspect pocket with a purpose. Sensing my urgency, he looked and quickly grabbed the offending item and stuffed it deeper in his pockets. In their laughter, the Marinos didn't seem to catch it and for that I was happy. The last thing I needed was for a few large country boys to get pissed that Foggdog was so blatantly hooking up with their little sister while they toiled in the fields. I wondered how they dealt with this little arrangement on days when I wasn't there.

After a moment, the laughter died down and we got back to business. Ed introduced me to his sons, oldest-to-youngest: Ed Junior (whom they simply called "Junior"), Mike, and Rob. After shaking each of their hands, we got down to business.

"So, why'd you call us down here, Pop?" asked Junior.

"I called you down here because Ray here is going to explain to you why we're about to plan an all-out assault on the food camps." Ed looked at me. "Tell 'em exactly how you told me and I'm sure they'll all agree. We're in."

CHAPTER SEVENTEEN

The water in the lake was clear, clean and always plentiful. Being at the top of a hill, I imagined the only thing feeding it was rainwater, but perhaps there was some sort of underground spring as well. I imagined the water was probably drinkable, though we had always boiled every ounce we used. Having the lake on the property seemed like a nice novelty when we moved in, though I can count on one hand the number of times we used it before the crisis happened. Now we seemed to go there daily – especially to irrigate the crops.

Charlotte would always take Anna up to the lake under the impression that she would be helping out. But she largely spent her time swimming. We tried our best to give her enough occasions to just let loose, have fun, and enjoy the innocence of being a child. It was so easy to despair.

Charlotte and Anna had left for the lake and I sat down in the office amongst a few new books I had picked up from the library using Mrs. Quigley's key. I opened up the first book, Sun Tzu's <u>The Art Of War</u>, not really knowing what to expect. It was always the first book that came to mind – generals read it, football coaches read it, and they all swore by the wisdom within. It didn't seem like the kind of book to read cover-to-cover, so I scanned through most of it, not really understanding what it was that I was looking for.

"Anyone who excels in defeating his enemies triumphs before his enemy's threat becomes real."

Leaning back in the chair, I reflected on that phrase for a moment. The office was quiet except for the gentle breeze through the trees outside and the occasional bird-chirping that came through the open window. Resting on the desk was my loaded shotgun, at the ready should any intruder come up the road or burst through the door. I wondered if I'd ever go anywhere again without the protection of a firearm. There was certainly an ongoing real threat, but for the most part that came from the chance that thieves or desperate vagrants might think this place an opportunity to plunder.

Outside of that omnipresent threat, my concern was even broader. What would happen if the military gave up its foreign incursions and hundreds of thousands of soldiers came home? Would they be used to control areas of domestic insurgency and crime? Would they perhaps be sent to relieve the guards at the labor camps, who, according to Art Brady weren't really trained guards anyway? The government clearly had a wide-ranging control over the population in the food camps, but what about the people who were out there on their own? Maybe they'd steal our crops in the name of taxation. Maybe one day they would knock on our door and force us to go the food camps ourselves, or perhaps worse. Maybe one day they would show up with guns, and not bother to knock at all.

The one sure-thing was that I did not want to sit around and wait to find out. Sun Tzu's passage only heightened my sense of urgency further. My transformation was nearly complete. Art's appearance had awakened me to the incredible wrongs being perpetrated on friends and neighbors just a few miles down the road. The map on the wall still contained all the pushpins with the locations where we had collected the weapons needed for the assault. Recruiting Colin and the Marinos gave us a sense of team and purpose, not to mention confirmation that our goals were noble and worthwhile.

And now this one nugget of wisdom found in an ancient tome provided the guidance for when to go about doing what we had to do. Our mission must be planned and undertaken as soon as possible.

I tucked the book away for the time being and focused on some other texts I had removed from the library. When Mrs. Quigley handed me that key, I thought of how much pleasure it would give Anna, knowing that while all of the other stores had closed down she would always have access to her books. I remember taking out those first few books on farming and survivalist techniques that had proved to be extremely useful. But as I sat there staring at my latest stack of books on guerrilla warfare techniques and weaponry, I realized that Mrs. Quigley's simple gesture of friendship had gone above and beyond anything either of us could have envisioned.

I thought about poor Mrs. Quigley and how she must be doing in the camps. Clearly she was in no shape for manual labor or to resist tyranny. I knew she would approve of our plan to free her since her name was on one of the cards, and I hoped we might see each other again soon.

My studies continued into the afternoon. Charlotte and Anna returned from the lake and spent a few hours in Anna's playroom as Charlotte taught long-division, a topic I remember despising. But Charlotte had a way of keeping Anna alert and engaged and I couldn't help but wonder how great school might have been for me if I, too, had teachers like Charlotte.

The afternoon slowly transformed into evening, and then night. It was a significant ride to the camps that would take hours on bicycles, so I knew that I shouldn't expect Mitch and Foggdog to return anytime soon. Even so, I was beginning to get a little nervous. I started thinking the worst – what would happen if they were caught spying? Would they be captured or hurt? Would they be questioned?

For a minute, I thought about that scenario, and while I had complete faith in Mitch's ability to know the importance of withholding where he had lived over the past few months, I wasn't as confident in Foggdog. It was yet another thing for which we hadn't planned or practiced and I didn't even trust that Foggdog would know better than to just give up any information they wanted.

As it grew dark, it started to worry me more and more. After sharing my concerns with Charlotte, it was decided that we should just treat it like a normal night. I would go up and begin the first watch early while she would hang out with Anna and put her to bed. I sat up in the bedroom, as usual, though now I had a rifle, a shotgun, a handgun with a silencer attachment and a sniper's rifle in the room. I don't think I would have ever used the sniper's rifle, but Mitch seemed to think he knew how to use one so we kept it upstairs in the makeshift watchtower. Besides, the scope was pretty powerful and if I ever saw movement, I would sometimes grab the sniper rifle and use the scope to get a better look.

The wait began and I hoped that there was no legitimacy to my nervousness. A million possibilities went through my head, including that maybe my friends were lying in a ditch somewhere after being caught spying.

One hour went by, then two. I started wondering whether or not I could pull a full night shift on my own, and at what point was I going to truly get concerned for the well-being of my friends. Truthfully, that point had already come and gone. I was worried.

Just as I convinced myself that my concern was real and worthy, I saw a bobbing head appear over the ridge. It was a cyclist, making his way up the hill toward the house. I grabbed the sniper's rifle and peered through the powerful scope.

It was Mitch. I could finally breathe easy. Putting the rifle down, I instinctively pocketed the handgun and headed downstairs. Charlotte heard me coming and her head picked up over the back-end of the couch. "They're back," I whispered.

"Thank God."

I went out the side door to meet them, but it was only Mitch. Then I remembered the first time they arrived on bikes and figured Foggdog was just lagging behind and would be appearing momentarily.

"I was beginning to worry about you guys," I called out to Mitch.

"They got him," he said. *"They got Foggdog."*

We came inside to the office, and I now sat at the desk feeling defeated. So sure was I that Mitch and Foggdog would be able to quietly spy on the campground from the nearby wooded hills that I never even thought about the possibility of them being captured. I have used the term "worried sick," before but never in proper context because now I knew what it was like to be truly worried sick. Our friend was now in the grasp of the enemy and who knew how long it might be before they were knocking on our doorstep?

"We should have planned for this," I said. "Why didn't I plan for this?"

"He's just going to melt right in with the crowd," Mitch said. "I really don't think we have to worry."

I was still worried. So much so that it was likely visible on my face because Mitch continued to explain.

"I saw him being walked in to the camp. He wasn't cuffed or shackled and he wasn't being held at gunpoint. He was just walking alongside the guard as though they were leading him in. I think he just told them that he was hungry and wanted to find shelter at the camp."

It was a likely story, though I struggled to believe that Foggdog could think so quickly on his feet. This is a guy who had a history of getting caught cheating on multiple girlfriends for precisely that reason.

"Maybe this can work to our advantage," Mitch continued. "Maybe he will alert some people on the inside that we are on our way."

"Foggdog opening his mouth in that camp is the last thing we need," I exclaimed. That seemed to be a pretty fair statement because Mitch had no rebuttal.

Charlotte joined us in the office, noticing that attendance at this meeting was one person short. "He went to bed already?" she assumed.

"No," I said. "It's a little worse."

Mitch explained once again exactly how it had happened.

"It was weird on the ride down. We didn't see anything the whole way – not a car or bike, not a soul. It was almost eerie. But as we got closer, we became a little nervous about the possibility of getting caught. So we split up. I entered the woods from the North side and he went over towards the West. I found a great spot where I could see everything – the camp, the farm, the watchtowers, everything. Even better was that there was no way I could be detected up there. The leaves are still few enough for me to see through, but thick enough that nobody could possibly see me from the camps.

"I sat there for a couple of hours taking notes about the things I saw." Mitch looked over at his backpack and nodded. "In there are maps of the camp and notes on the schedule they were on – the shifts of the tower guards, what times the workers left for the fields, when they took breaks and when they returned.

"After about two hours of sitting there collecting info, I saw some men coming down the road. There were two of them and they seemed to just be chatting away as they strolled along. I almost didn't even notice who it was, but he kept staring up into the woods. For a second, I thought they had seen me but then I realized that it was him! It was Foggdog! They just strolled into the camp all nice and fine as if it was no big deal. He walked into a main building and out of view, and I didn't see him at all after that. I stayed there for probably another hour before I decided that I needed to go and make sure that his bike was not in clear view. So I ditched my post and got to my bike. I had to be really careful because I didn't want to wind up in the same place as he was. I kept wondering what you would think if neither of us came home tonight.

"Anyway, I found his bike right on the side of the road – exactly where he probably planned on going into the woods, if he ever really went in the woods."

"What did you do with it?" I asked.

"I thought about ghost riding it home, but 15 miles with a bike like that in the dark sounded a little too daunting," Mitch explained. "So, I just threw it back in the woods a bit and made sure it wasn't visible from the road."

The room got quiet. The news was terrible, but there was really nothing more to discuss. The situation at hand was what it was and there was nothing we could really do. I wondered if Foggdog might be able to escape from the camp, like Art had, and if he would go back to look for his bike. That seemed unlikely given his general malaise and laziness. He would certainly miss Katie after a few days, but he would also expect us to come to his rescue at some point.

I couldn't think about it any longer and just wanted to move on and keep my mind off Foggdog in the labor camp.

"Let's open the bag," I said.

Over the next hour, we went through all of the information Mitch had taken down. His map was incredible – practically a work of art. The detail was amazing, each tent and trailer drawn in shocking 3-D, outlined by the imposing fence and the watchtower.

"Nice drawing," I noted.

"Thanks."

"Where is the entrance?" I asked. "And the building where they took Foggdog?"

"I couldn't finish, but it's over here," he said, pointing to a general location on the map.

I sighed lightly in frustration.

"Maybe if you focused less on the detail, Van Gogh, and more on the information, you would have been able to finish."

We moved on to Mitch's notes. He had written down a whole schedule of the goings-on at the camp, but that seemed incomplete as well.

"Once Foggdog was captured, I couldn't pay much attention,"

Mitch admitted.

"Ok," I surmised, attempting to assemble this information in my brain into something useful. There was a lot there, and perhaps we could use some of it to begin formulating a plan.

"We need more," Mitch admitted.

"Yeah, I think we need more, too," I agreed. We hesitated for a moment, thinking about going back for another round of reconnaissance. "How safe do you feel going back?" I asked.

"I never saw anyone in the woods and I had a great spot to sit and gather info. I have no idea how he got caught. I hate to seem naïve about it, but spying on that camp was simple. "

I thought about Charlotte and about how she might survive if Mitch and I went down to the camp and got caught, or worse – what if we were killed?

"How bad were the people down there?"

"Awful," Mitch said. "Just awful. All of them wore matching gray jumpsuits like the one Art was wearing. They were skinny and dirty, and looked absolutely downtrodden and depressed. Everyone's heads were down and they were marched out to the fields, chaperoned by men with guns. It was terrible."

I thought of poor Mrs. Quigley and hoped she was still alive somewhere down at the camp. I had a sudden desire to tell her how her gift, a simple key, had made such a difference for us. Liberty Gulch was full of people just like Mrs. Quigley, who undoubtedly were in a dangerous predicament they couldn't possibly have foreseen. Many of them had filled out an index card, allowing a complete stranger access to their home and their possessions in the hopes that someone might come and save them. I couldn't let them down.

"Tomorrow morning," I concluded. "We leave early tomorrow morning."

Mitch nodded in affirmation.

It had been easy to talk Charlotte into approving our plan. If anything went wrong, she was to go to the Marinos and alert them to what happened. I was confident that Ed Marino would see to it that Charlotte and Anna were safe and secure. But I was hoping it would never get that far.

Just before dawn, Mitch and I took off on our bicycles down the hill and began the 17 mile ride to Maly Farms. We were very careful to keep an eye out on the roads so that we wouldn't run into bandits or perhaps even officials from the camp.

Mitch was very familiar with the route, even though he had only traveled it once before. Once we got close enough, we stashed the bikes and carefully made our way through the woods, up the hill to Mitch's spot, where I first laid my eyes on the camp.

The picture Mitch had drawn didn't do justice to the sheer scope of the camp as seen from up on the hill just to the north. I let out a gasp at the sight of it.

"I know," Mitch said. "I felt the same way."

For the next few hours, we sat there filling in the missing pieces. It was amazing how structured everything was. All of the things Mitch had witnessed the day before happened at the same exact time the day after. They marched out to the fields at the same time, they took breaks at the same time, they marched back at the same time. The guards moved in patterns, taking turns watching over their captives. The guard in the tower was relieved of duty every hour on the hour.

At one point, we saw a car enter the camp through the front gate. "I forgot to mention that," Mitch said. "It stayed about a half-hour last time and then took off. I guess I forgot because shortly after it left I saw Foggdog being walked in."

"Hmm... listen," I observed.

"What? I don't hear anything."

"Exactly... the car doesn't run on gas. It's electric. Sorta makes sense if you think about it. Maybe Foggdog didn't hear him coming and they caught him."

I saw the eureka-moment cross Mitch's face.

"Dammit, how did I not see that?"

"Maybe because you're not a professional spy?"

I could tell Mitch wasn't accepting that as an excuse, so I helped him further.

"Even if you figured out that it was an electric car there was nothing you could do to help him. He was going to get caught no matter what."

That seemed to appease Mitch's sense of guilt, and we continued to focus on the camp. We sat for hours in the relative quiet and observed. Mitch finished his map, though the rest of it was done in less vivid detail and more attention was given to specific landmarks than to artistic flair.

The day was long and tedious as we sat and watched what had become the wretched every-day life of our friends and neighbors. There were no more picnics or sporting events like the ones shown on television just a few months ago. The camp that was put in place to help feed the people had now essentially become a prison.

The men came in from the fields for what seemed to be the last time for the day, and we started thinking about heading back home. The last thing I wanted to do was make Charlotte worry, so we started packing up the bags. As Mitch stowed the map into the bag, I kept an eye on the camp looking for something specific. It didn't take me long to find it.

"Look," I said to Mitch, who stood up as he slung the backpack on his shoulder. "There."

Sure enough there was one figure amongst the many laborers who walked with a bit more pep in his step and seemed a little cleaner and healthier than the others.

"Foggdog," Mitch identified.

It was gut-wrenching to see him out there among the workers when just a day earlier he had been free and among his friends. Despite his laziness and regular disappearing to go see his girlfriend, he was still a good friend and it was hard to see him in such a situation.

"We have to do this soon," Mitch said.

"I know."

We rode home without incident, arriving well before the time Charlotte might begin to worry. After all that biking and climbing I was completely exhausted. Charlotte had picked up the slack in the garden that day along with Anna and they were tired, too. We all slept well that night despite the event which loomed on the more immediate horizon as each day passed. Somehow, we slept.

CHAPTER EIGHTEEN

Colin was the first to show up at the doorstep as we began to plan and train for the mission ahead. Part of me wondered if he would have a change of heart and not show up. Perhaps last week, I would have welcomed that idea. But now that we were going ahead full-steam with this, I was certainly glad to see him. Ed and his entire family, Katie included, showed up shortly after.

I wasn't ready to deliver the unpleasant news to Katie and part of me was hoping that she wouldn't be coming to the house. Certainly, she wouldn't miss an opportunity to see Foggdog and I knew her father wouldn't want to leave her home alone. So, there she was.

I greeted them at the door, immediately introducing Colin, Mitch, Charlotte and Anna before hearing the question I was afraid to hear, yet knew would come.

"Hi, Mr. Stanton," she said joyously, as if she were excitedly looking forward to visiting her boyfriend. "Where's Jimmy? Is he home?"

The look on my face must have given up the answer before I spit out the words, "No, I'm afraid not."

Her hands immediately went to her mouth and she began crying, apparently thinking the worst of the worst.

"No, no, no," I said as Ed Marino immediately threw his arm around his daughter in attempt to console her, while looking at me for an explanation. "He's fine, he's healthy," I assured her, which got her to calm down a bit and give me her full attention. "He's just not... *here*."

The look of confusion on everyone's face demanded an explanation, but I knew it would be better if we moved into the house first, so I invited everyone in. We had arranged the living room in such a fashion to accommodate all of the guests, with an area in the front set up so that we could present our findings. We sat Katie down on the same couch where Art Brady had taken his final rest, though I decided to withhold that fact from her at this moment.

"Two days ago, Mitch and Fog... um... Jimmy, went down to gather information on the camp. We wanted to do some recon so that we could best devise a plan." I looked at all their faces and none of them seemed to be exhibiting a look of disgust over that decision, which gave me confidence that we were all still on the same page.

"The guys split up to get a couple of different angles at the camp and to decrease the chances of both of them getting caught. Mitch found a good spot in the woods and after a few hours he saw Foggdog being led into the camp; he had been captured." A collective gasp echoed through the room.

"He's okay, though," I quickly added. "We don't know how he was captured, but he walked right into the camp unhurt and unfazed and when we went back down to do some more investigating, we saw him working right alongside everybody else."

That seemed to put everyone at ease for the time being as they were happy to hear that Jimmy was healthy and safe.

"That's it," Katie said resolutely, as she looked at her father. "We have to save Jimmy, Dad. We have to save him right now."

If anything, his daughter's predicament only solidified Ed Marino's intention to join the assault. And as long as Ed was in, his three boys were in. And as the doorbell rang, we were about to find out that it didn't end there either.

Five burly men stood at my doorstep – men I had never seen before. If this were any other day, and these men had shown up at our house with nobody there, they would have scared me to death. But on this day, I could almost sense what they were there for as the Marino boys soon confirmed.

"I hope you don't mind, Ray," Junior chimed in. "But we invited some friends."

The men all shook hands and gave each other guy-hugs as they entered my living room, which was now standing-room-only. We were introduced to them – Kevin, Tim, George, Pete, and Alex.

"I'm sorry," Junior said. "These guys are all old friends of ours who have been going at it alone the past few months. They are very dependable and eager to help us out."

I was a tiny bit skeptical, as I hadn't met any of these men before. But we definitely needed the help and I was going to look at it with an open mind. "So you boys know what we're fighting for then?" I asked.

They all nodded.

"Why don't we start there?" Ed requested. "Maybe you can tell us again about how Art Brady showed up at your house and all that. We tried to tell them the story, but I don't know that it had as much flavor as when you told it."

"We're here, ain't we?" remarked one of the men – it could have been Pete or Tim. I wasn't sure which one was which anymore. I always had a difficult time remembering names.

"Well, let's just start there and then we can move on to something else," Ed said.

"Ok."

I stood in front of the room and tried to repeat the story I had told to Colin, at gunpoint in his uncle's kitchen. It was the same story I tried to plug life into when I sat on Ed Marino's porch, and then again to his sons minutes after. It was still fresh in my mind; I think it will always be fresh in my mind.

There were no questions asked and everyone seemed intensely focused and I could sense everyone was on board. So, after I finished the story, I segued deftly into the initial purpose for today's meeting – to plan the assault on the camp.

Mitch helped me affix his map to the mantle over our fireplace, where I pointed out the details of the camp – the entranceways and buildings, the watchtower, the tents and trailers, the barns and the fields.

I went through it all, and then I focused on the schedule that we had ascertained. During the day only one person manned the watchtower at a time. The field workers were constantly guarded by two men with shotguns. There were guards patrolling the living areas at all times, and we never could get a handle on exactly how many were stationed inside the main building at the entranceway to the camp. We estimated a total of fifteen to twenty guards.

"Now, correct me if I'm wrong," Colin observed, "but we are

what? One, two, three, four," he began counting.

"Twelve," Mitch concluded. "We are now twelve."

"Thirteen," chimed the voice of Katie Marino. "We are thirteen. If Jimmy is in that camp, then I'm going with you."

I could sense the shock in Ed Marino as he looked at his daughter, who seemed as though she wouldn't be taking "no" for an answer. Before he could get a word out, Katie pressed her case forward.

"No, Dad. You know I can shoot. I can shoot better than anyone in this room," she brazenly claimed to the "Harrumphs" of some of the men.

At this, Ed stood up – rising from his seat in defense of his daughter. "Actually, boys, she can. Katie was the girls' state champion in both skeet and target shooting." He said it with a mix of the pride any parent might have for the successes of their child, but also with caution for the fact that he had just practically supported the notion of his only daughter joining in on our assault.

He looked her in the eye and could tell he wasn't going to win this argument, at least not now. So he turned back to me, hoping to change the subject.

"What else do we have, Ray?" he asked.

"We have a few other advantages," I said. "The guards seem more intent on keeping people in the camp than protecting the camp from an assault from the outside. And one of the things that Art had mentioned just before he died was that the guards seemed untrained – more like they were management-type bureaucrats forced to take up guns in order to keep the camps in line.

"One potential bright side of Jimmy's capture is that maybe he can make a few people aware that we are on our way and they'll be prepared to take up arms alongside us. We all know Jimmy has trouble keeping his mouth shut."

"Tell us about these weapons," Junior asked.

"Weapons," I answered. "We have a lot of weapons." I knew that I was looking across a sea of people who were all well armed in that almost everyone in the area had a rifle, if not for hunting then at least for scaring the bears away when they got too close. Other than taking a few shots at rabbits with Mitch's pistol, I had no idea what I was doing. But that wasn't the image that I needed to convey in this room, so I did my best to fake as though I knew what I was talking about.

"We have shotguns, rifles, handguns, pistols, and all the ammo that you can carry. Then there are the live grenades and the sniper rifle," I said.

Katie immediately perked up. "Sniper rifle?" she asked. Perhaps I shouldn't have mentioned it.

"Don't get any thoughts in your head, Katie," her father objected.

"But Dad," she pressed. "I can sit up in the woods and just shoot if necessary. We can build a perch," she said.

"There's no need to build a perch," Mitch interjected. "You can sit on the hill in the woods. It's well-covered and you'll never be seen. There are plenty of spots where you can get a full view of the camp from up there. That's how we drew the map in the first place."

Ed Marino shot Mitch a glare that would have probably physically injured a lesser man, but Mitch stood firm.

"Look," he said. "We had assumed all along that someone would have to use that sniper rifle and we discussed using the woods as cover. Besides, physically assembling a perch in a tree is likely to get us caught from the noise alone. And if Katie is as good of a shot as you are saying, maybe she should be the one using that gun. Is anybody else here as qualified?"

Nobody raised their hand – perhaps it was because they knew they were not a good shot, or maybe they didn't want to risk insulting Ed Marino. Either way, the room grew quiet.

"Ed," I said with a sigh. "Maybe this isn't such a bad idea. If she is far away from the action, she'll be able to escape if something bad happens. Frankly, if that were to happen, I was hoping that someone would be able to get back and report it to Charlotte and Anna. I am scared as hell at the thought of them going at it alone if something were to happen to us, but if they had Katie with them? I like their chances a lot better."

Ed mulled it over as the room waited. It was understandable that a father would not want to lead his daughter into combat, but if she was as good as they said, she might be a formidable asset in this battle. And with the stakes so high, we couldn't afford not to use everything we had.

"Ok," he said. "Fine. But your role is sniper and nothing else. If anything happens, you do not go into the camp, you run away. Do we have a deal?"

"Yes, daddy," she said, and gave him a hug. I never thought I'd see someone so happy about being allowed to join a battle where bullets would be flying and people could be dying. And she was doing it all for *Foggdog*. He was trapped in a labor camp, but in the moment I was almost happy for him. It was pretty obvious that he finally found a girl who truly loved him.

After going over all of the details so that everyone knew what we were up against, it was time to head out back and check out the toys. We couldn't really shoot off countless live rounds because the echo would surely draw attention. Of course, all anyone wanted to do was check out our sniper in action.

We stood on the side porch near the swing. The laundry was hung on a makeshift line from the garage to a tree out back. Charlotte had just washed the sheets and they blew gently in the breeze.

"I need to make sure the sights are properly aligned," Katie explained as she held the sniper rifle in her hands. "How much ammo do we have?"

"Two boxes," I said, handing them over. "And one seems a lot lighter than the other."

The boxes were sealed with old scotch tape. Katie took the lighter box and, cutting the tape with her fingernail, opened it. "Two shells," she observed. "That should at least help me align the sights."

We went to the backyard and Katie looked around for a target.

"Would you like me to get a few soda cans or bottles or something?" I asked, figuring those would do the job.

"Heh," she chuckled. "And what would happen if I missed?" she asked. "How would I know how to adjust the sights if I couldn't see the result of the shot?" It was a stupid question and I was glad that none of the men had heard me ask it or I would have felt really dumb.

"Are you in love with any of those sheets?" she asked, pointing to the ones drying on the line.

I wasn't sure that we had back-ups, but this seemed like our best option for a target right now, and if it meant that I would be sleeping with a sheet that had a few holes in it, so be it. "Let's do it."

Katie went to the sheet in the middle, where the line had bowed at its lowest. She took some dirt from the ground and drew a little circle on it. As she let go of the sheet, it flapped in the wind.

"We're going to have to do something about this wind," I

commented.

"Maybe we can find another guy and get you to hold the two ends down while I shoot," she said.

"Fuck, no" I said.

She chuckled. "Relax, I was just kidding," she said and patted me on the shoulder. Even in the face of the situation, Katie showed a remarkable ability to retain her sense of humor. No wonder Foggdog liked her so much.

It seemed somewhat ironic that initially he was ready to go to the camps, but meeting her kept him from going and then he wound up there anyway. Maybe it was meant to be.

We gathered some rocks and used them to hold the sheet down. Then she walked back about fifty yards or so. Katie loaded the rifle and took a prone stance on the ground. "This is going to be pretty loud," she said, and got ready to shoot.

She was right.

The first shot sounded like an explosion, followed by echoes in the trees and mountains far away. I looked over at Ed and Mitch. "As long as we only fire a couple shots, they'll just think we're hunting," Ed said, as if he read my mind in wondering if the shots could be detected.

Katie walked over to the sheet, inspecting the results. She had missed dead-center by about three inches to the right, and one inch high. It seemed like a pretty decent shot to me, but she wasn't very happy about it.

"This is no good," she remarked.

"It looks pretty close to me," I added.

"Yeah, from fifty yards maybe. I'm guessing I'll be what, a hundred yards from the watchtower? Maybe more?" she asked.

"Yeah, sounds about right."

"A 3-inch miss from 50 yards is a six-inch miss from a hundred. A six-inch miss when you're aiming for a man's head will miss completely. I'm going to have to shoot another one."

She walked back to her spot and began adjusting the rifle. Watching her at work, it was easy to lose any reservation I may have had about allowing a woman to fight alongside us. It was amazing to see and a minute later she was back in the prone position and firing her second shot.

The blast rang out once more, but since we were expecting it this time it didn't seem so bad. Still, I was hoping that she wouldn't have to fire a third. One shot, maybe two shots and I could buy the hunting storyline. Three shots or more? I didn't know.

We approached the sheet again and, from a distance, I didn't see a mark at all. It made me a little nervous at first as if maybe she had missed the sheet completely. But as we got close, I could tell why – it was because the shot had hit dead-center, right on the dirt-mark Katie had drawn on it moments ago.

"That'll do," she said, poking her finger through the hole.

"I'd say so."

The other men clapped and whistled at the shooting display we had just witnessed, sincerely impressed at the skill of our new soldier. I think we were all glad that she was on our side and not sitting in one of those watchtowers with her sights trained on us.

Katie picked up the sniper rifle and the remaining box of ammo and we all congregated around the picnic table in the backyard. Resting the rifle on the table, she opened the remaining box – perhaps to inspect it or to count the shells.

The rest of the men stood around as Katie gave a strange look at the box, now opened.

"This is all the ammo we have for the sniper rifle?" she asked.

"Yes," I replied. "I think so. Those were the only boxes we found."

"Shit," she said, tossing the box across the table, its contents spilling out all over the lawn as we all stood shocked at her reaction.

"What's the matter?" Ed Marino asked his daughter. I was glad he was the one to muster up the courage to ask her, because I sure as hell wasn't.

"Those rounds will not fit this rifle. Those are different rounds in that box – it's not what it says on the label," she claimed as we all stood around wondering what that really meant, before she summed it up for us. "I have no more ammunition for the sniper rifle!"

Her face began to bunch up and turn red, as if she were about to burst out in tears but was holding it in. Her hands eventually covered her face, and she stormed away along the back of the house. The entire Marino family chased after her, father and brothers.

The rest of us sat at the table, unwilling to get involved in family business.

"Boy, that girl can shoot, eh?" one of the new guys asked – I think it was Kevin.

"Hell, yeah," another one of them agreed.

I went over and grabbed the box, not really knowing what it was that I was looking at or reading. I picked up one of the shells off the lawn and inspected it. Sure enough, it looked nothing like the picture on the box. What dumb luck.

Instead of looking at the current predicament as something to lament, I decided to turn it into a problem we needed to solve.

"So," I began. "Does anyone know where we can get a few bullets for a sniper rifle?"

It almost sounded as if I was joking, and I half-expected someone to laugh at the thought. But one of the new boys spoke up almost immediately.

"I might," said the voice. The man's name was Pete, and he seemed to be the quietest and most reserved of the bunch. He was the only one, for whatever reason, whose name I remembered after being introduced. He hadn't spoken a word since entering my home, but here he was potentially solving our problem.

"Ok," I said with a shrug of my shoulders, as if anticipating an explanation.

"There's a guy about five miles from here – a real loner, former military man. I'd call him a survivalist, I guess. He just lives off the land and I only met him but once. He was real nice to me, but I got the sense that he was well versed in weaponry."

"How'd you get that?" I asked.

"We were just at Sonny's Bar, chattin', and he got a little tipsy. He started talking about some of the missions he went on in the first Iraq War and how he was shootin' guys down, pickin' them off from hundreds of yards away. I assumed that meant he was a pretty good shot. Anyway, he tells me he lives on this ranch by himself and that he loves his country, but he was afraid of her direction and how he was preparing for the day when the shit hit the fan."

"And you think he might have what we need?"

"I don't know. Just listening to what the guy had to say, I'd guess he's got a whole fortress built up there. He was incredibly distrusting of the government and seemed to think that one day he might have to defend himself against them. I'd guess he'd have just about any weapon you need. Maybe we could even get him to join us?"

"I'd be happy if he just had shells for that rifle," I said. "And I guess there's only one way to find that out."

CHAPTER NINETEEN

Riding up the unknown survivalist's driveway on bicycles was not the movie-entrance I thought I'd be making in a situation like this. The Marino brothers had come along with us, but they waited at the bottom of the driveway. We didn't want to appear as though we were looking to start a fight, so it was decided that I would go up with Pete since he was the one who had met our contact before, and I was the one with the money.

We laid the bicycles down at the top of the gravel driveway and I pulled the backpack off of my shoulders, holding it by the strap. Pete and I stood there a moment, taking in the sight before us.

The house was more like a cabin. It was built out of wood which may have once been a happier color, but was now a weathered shade of dark gray. The windows were small and very dark, revealing none of the inside of the house. There was a detached garage, essentially the same construction type as the home itself. To say it was imposing was an understatement. I imagined that whoever lived here didn't get many trick-or-treaters on Halloween.

"Who lives here?" I asked. "Boo Radley?"

"I don't remember his name," Pete said, completely unaware of my literary reference.

The silence was noticeable, as if even the birds dared not chirp in these trees. The only noise I heard was Pete's footsteps as he made his way across the gravel towards the door. I was shocked at his fearlessness as I, myself, was scared to death. He was a good 20 feet ahead of me and about 5 feet from the front door when we heard the raspy, gruff voice of our host.

"You're trespassing," he grunted, causing us to turn and face the man now standing in front of the detached garage with some type of automatic machine gun in his hands.

My first reaction was to drop the bag and take a slow step back. I immediately regretted coming here – maybe this was a stupid idea after all. I looked over at Pete, who apparently expected a more cordial greeting because he was visibly shaking with fear.

"What the fuck are you doing here?" the man asked, holding the gun steadily at me but shifting his gaze between us. He wore full camouflage and looked as though he had been sitting there waiting for us to arrive. His hair was typical military – high and tight – and his face bore a sort of crescent-shaped scar below his right eye. He looked like he had been through a war and, of course, he had.

Again I looked at Pete, who didn't appear at all ready to answer the question laid before him, despite being the one whose bright idea it was to come here.

Sensing any further delay might cause us to look as though our intentions were something less than noble, I decided I had to do the talking. "Sir, I'm very sorry, sir. We didn't mean to startle you."

"Startle me?" he shot back. "You think I'm startled? Look at your friend here. I'd say he's the startled one; the boy's about to piss his pants."

I almost laughed at that comment, because I thought it was actually true. Pete, in fact, looked as though he was ready to piss his pants. This was the second time in the last few weeks that I found myself one itchy trigger-finger away from death. Perhaps I was getting used to it.

"Maybe those three boys you left down at the end of the path will be startled when they start hearin' some machine gun rounds. What do you think?" he asked.

He was clearly letting us know he knew exactly what was going on at all times and he was the one in control. With the machine gun leveled at our chests, I'm not so sure that was ever in question anyway.

"Sir," I decided to change the subject. "We are in dire need of a special kind of ammunition for a certain kind of rifle. My friend Pete here knew you from Sonny's Bar, and thought maybe you could help us out."

The man gave a long stare at Pete, who appeared to be getting a little more comfortable with the situation. At least, he no longer appeared ready to wet himself. After a moment, the man began to nod at Pete in affirmation.

"I haven't been down to Sonny's in months," he snipped, leveling the gun once more at Pete, who immediately cringed up where he stood. "But... you do look a little familiar."

"Y-Yes," Pete finally mustered, though in a definitive stutter.

The man's mouth seemed to draw up in a smile, though he didn't lower his weapon. Instead, he changed the subject. "What's in the bag?" he asked me, referring to the backpack that was now on the ground.

There was no sense in lying.

"Cash," I said. "So that I could pay you for what I need."

He seemed to chuckle at that notion. "Cash?" he asked. "You think I need fucking cash? That shit's worth less than my stash of toilet paper." I couldn't really argue with him on that point. "What kind of rounds are we talking about?" he asked.

I lowered my hands slowly and moved them towards my pocket, giving our captor a quizzical look as if to ask permission to reach in. He nodded – permission granted. I removed the folded up empty ammo box from my pocket and offered it to him. He finally lowered his rifle as if accepting our presence, though he cautiously took the box from my hand. After taking a few steps back, with one finger still on the trigger of his lowered gun, he read the box.

"This story just keeps getting better and better," he said. "You boys plan on doing some hunting with these?"

"No," I replied.

"Good, cuz it'd be a waste to kill a good deer with a slug like this – you'd ruin the meat."

I couldn't tell if he was being serious or not. If he was, then maybe he just took us for a couple of local idiots who didn't know what they were doing. Maybe he was still trying to figure us out – who we were, why we were on his land or what our true intentions were.

When he waited a few moments without responding, I knew he wasn't going to go forward without more information. However, he didn't seem like the kind of person who would positively respond to the heart-wrenching story of Art Brady. Frankly, I was getting tired of telling it – especially while at gunpoint. So I gave him the short version instead.

"The government has turned the food camps into labor camps. Many of our neighbors and close friends are there – suffering and dying. So, we're planning to organize an assault to liberate the camp."

At this, our captor next spoke with a tone of disbelief, "No shit."

"No shit," I responded confidently, trying to stare through him so that he would take me seriously.

He stood momentarily as if contemplating his next move.

"So, you're going to go shoot up a government labor camp," he said, looking for affirmation as if he couldn't believe his ears.

"You're welcome to join us," I invited.

He chuckled. "I'm a survivor and this is my land. I'll stay here and defend it against anyone," he said before laughing again, this time with more emphasis and exuberance. "But I ain't so fuckin' stupid as to attack the government of the United States!" he said, before spitting some tobacco on the gravel driveway. He shouldered his weapon. "Follow me."

Picking the backpack off the ground, I followed the man across the driveway toward the garage. Pete walked behind me, still flustered from the experience of having a machine gun leveled at him by a man who seemed to have the fortitude to use it.

The garage had two car-entrances, but looked deep enough that it might fit two cars back-to-back on each side. Inside was very dark, with the only light emanating from small windows above. We were led into a space that appeared big enough for a car, but was blocked in all directions by metal shelving.

Once in the garage, the man nodded towards the empty space, apparently wanting us to move into the room before he closed the door behind us. Upon doing so, the room grew even darker.

"Wait right here," he said. "And don't do nothin' stupid." He looked up towards the ceiling of the garage where we could barely make out the form of another man in dark clothing perched in the rafters. He held up a hand gun so that we could see it. We understood. We weren't going anywhere.

The man walked back beyond the shelves outside of our vision. We could hear his footsteps shuffling around as if he were browsing the shelves of a department store. Finally, the sound of the steps grew progressively louder until the man reappeared, with two boxes in his hand.

He placed the boxes on the workbench, keeping his eyes on us the entire time. Even with back-up in the rafters, you could sense this man was trained militarily and he commanded control throughout the entire situation. I almost wished he would change his mind about joining us because, although I felt that we had a strong advantage in having the element of surprise, our complete lack of combat experience and training were certainly our most obvious weakness.

"So," he began, "What else you got in that bag?"

Apparently we were now in the negotiation phase, so I slung the bag from my shoulder and unzipped it. I had no idea what a box of ammunition was worth before the whole economy seemed to collapse, and since we hadn't made any recent purchases with all the stores being closed, I had even less of a clue what it would cost now.

Before I left the house earlier, I had looked at our stash of cash and thought about how much comfort it would give me to have a talented sniper in the woods while we launched our assault. I hadn't used any of this cash in months and it felt virtually worthless in my hands. Even so, I thought it should be worth *something*. It represented years of hard work from both me and Charlotte, toiling away in our old corporate offices believing there was no other way to live.

Looking at the money, I didn't think of how much a box of bullets would cost. Rather, I thought of how much of my stack of cash would I be willing to give up for the comfort of putting that sniper rifle in Katie's capable hands. How much was I willing to spend to help ensure that Anna's daddy would come home? How much did I want to leave behind should Anna's daddy not come home after the assault? The more I took, the more selfish I felt. So I cut about a quarter of the stack and brought it with me, thinking I could negotiate.

Perhaps I should have foreseen the situation a little bit better, because now he knew exactly how much I was willing to part with in order to get that ammo. So, I took the whole stack out of the bag.

"I assume this will do," I said, holding it out towards him.

He just started laughing, as if I had just told the funniest joke in the world. His laughter was echoed from the rafters as even the stealthy gunman above somehow found that funny. Eventually the laughter would die down and the bargainer on the floor got serious.

"I wouldn't trade a pair a' underwear for that stack of paper right there. That's all it is to me... paper. Please tell me you brought something else other than *that* with you, else you boys will be going home empty-handed."

"But sir," I began to explain.

"No, no, no," he cut me off before I could begin. "No 'buts'! What else you got?"

I thought quickly, but nothing was coming to mind. What could I give this man in return for the ammunition I needed so desperately?

"My bike," I said. "We rode here on bicycles and it's at the bottom of your driveway. How about that?"

"A bicycle?" he chuckled. "What are we in grade school here? You gonna throw in your Barbie doll next? There's only one thing in this world worthy of exchange," he explained. "And I see that you're married." At that statement, he nodded at my left hand which had the wedding ring Morris Roberts had graciously given me all those months ago – the one that fittingly replaced my original wedding ring that was now lying somewhere at the bottom of our lake.

Immediately lifting my hand, I placed my right hand over top of the ring as if to somehow guard it from his grasp. But after a momentary hesitation, I realized there was no other way.

"It's gold, I presume?" the man asked.

"Of course," I answered, slowly removing it from my ring finger, conscious of the fact that Morris had entrusted me as a guardian of this heirloom, and now I was trading it for bullets. I wondered if, under the circumstances, he would have done the same.

"On one condition," I added, which seemed to take him by surprise somewhat.

"What's that?"

"On the condition that I may return in a few days with another gold item, of equal or greater value, and exchange it for my ring back."

"This ain't no pawn shop," he said, and let the offer dangle in the air for a bit, probably not wanting to seem like he was giving in though eventually, he would. "But you got a deal."

"Thank you," I said with a sigh of relief. I held my hand out and he shook it. "I'll hold it at least a couple weeks, but if you're not back by then, I'm not responsible for it after that."

Walking over to the bench, he grabbed the boxes and then handed them over.

"Thank you," I said again.

"The pleasure was all mine," he answered. "Now get the hell off my property."

We happily obliged.

Walking down the long, gravel driveway I stashed the boxes of ammo into the backpack alongside the unused cash and realized it was time to deal with another issue.

"Pete?" I said calmly as could be.

"Yes," he answered in somewhat of a shameful tone, as if he knew that I was about to admonish him for his lack of courage.

"Pete, I'm not going to tell any of these guys what happened here today with you," I began. I could tell he drew a bit of relief from that statement. I continued speaking softly, "But we are going on a mission to assault the camp in a few days and there are going to be guns and there is going to be shooting this time." I stopped in my tracks and faced him, pointing at his chest. "And if you don't grow some fucking balls by then, I will shoot you in your fucking sleep before you step one foot on that battlefield, do you hear me? My daughter's life depends on this mission's success and I'll be damned if I'm going to put my trust in some pussy whose going to wet his fucking pants every time he sees a gun."

He looked surprised to hear me speak like that. I was a bit surprised myself and it made me wonder if this whole charade was beginning to take its toll on me as well. I had held it together really well so far – through the hard labor, the bad winter, the power-outage and the planning of an assault to free our friends. Maybe in the end, everyone would lose their edge.

After a moment, Pete nodded. "I'm sorry, Ray," he said. "It just took me by surprise is all. I'll be ready next time. Please don't tell the guys. Please don't," he pleaded. The threat of ridicule among men can often be a strong motivator.

"I won't," I said, satisfied that at least the problem had been addressed for the time being.

"Thank you."

We met our group at the end of the driveway, hopped back on the bikes and headed home. The deal was done, and we had our sniper back.

CHAPTER TWENTY

Over the next few days, we got down to the business of planning the assault. I had no real military training, but had somehow seemed to earn the trust of the men as a leader. It just happened that way, I don't know how. Maybe it was because of the way I told the story of Art Brady, or the way I negotiated for the sniper ammo, or the way I somehow found myself taking control of every situation. I'm not quite sure how I got that role, but it somehow landed squarely on my shoulders.

I always felt my hold on that position was tenuous at best and I knew that I could not afford to fracture any of the confidence the men had in me. It seemed of primary importance to always act tougher than I really was and exude the sense that I was in complete control, when inside I felt as though I was hurtling towards what might very well be my own death. Confidence was important, as I knew from my interaction with Pete. It wasn't only that I needed to have it myself, but I needed to instill it in others and I felt as though I could accomplish that by giving the impression that I had everything under control.

When it came to planning the assault, there were three men involved. Mitch had become pretty much my right-hand man. He beamed with confidence and never once questioned my authority in front of the men. In our planning stages he always politely offered suggestions and listened to explanations about specific details as we hammered them out. The third party was Ed Marino, the elder statesman of the Marino clan.

None of us in the room had military training, unless you count the hours of studying I was doing at night. People train for years to become military strategists and here I was trying to learn it in weeks, often reading by candlelight using the books from Mrs. Quigley's library.

Ed Marino was very outspoken at these meetings and though I was appreciative of his input, his opinions were usually rigid and it took a great deal of cajoling in order to move him in the direction we favored. Compounding the problem was that I knew that if Ed Marino decided to up and leave at any given point, along with him would go his sons, their friends, and our sniper. There was no way that Mitch, Colin and I were going to attack the camp on our own, no matter how good the plan.

We were especially at odds about our initial approach to the camp. Mitch and I wanted to wait for the electric car to make its daily run, entering and leaving the camp. Then, we would send one group out through the fields in my truck, securing those working in the field and arming them with our extra weapons. The watchtower was located in the front of the camp and the guards were not well-equipped for a shot of that distance – Katie's gun was a more advanced weapon than the ones the guards used in the tower. Even if they got a shot off, there was a good chance it wouldn't hit.

Ed wanted a completely different approach. He favored hijacking the electric car and loading it up with weapons. Then, we could just drive straight through the front door, overtake the guards and disburse the weapons to those people who weren't in the fields.

The positive to Ed's plan was that hijacking the car would probably give us easier access to driving straight into the camp without being noticed, while our entrance would be much louder.

For a number of days, we agreed to disagree and hoped that our continued spy-trips to the camps would help give us the right answer. At one time or another, every member of our entourage took a trip down to the camp to get familiar with the surroundings. We surveyed the front entrance and we made sure the guards were on the same schedule.

We even got Katie down there one afternoon to help pick out the best spot for her to set up. While there, she was also able to get a look at Foggdog, who kept on working day after day in the fields. Surely he knew we would come; only there was no real way to let him know when. It would sure be helpful if we could.

As I sat one evening trying to figure out a way to make a definitive argument to Ed about our approach to the camp, I began once again reading The Art of War. Whenever I needed answers, they seemed to jump off the pages.

"The best policy is to capture the state intact; it should be destroyed only if no other options are available."

Once it was spelled out for me in this fashion, it got my mind racing. We had no idea where the electric car was coming from on a day-to-day basis, and we had no way to track it (other than pedaling extremely fast on bicycles). Imagine if the car didn't make it to its destination one day. Surely, someone would wonder why and maybe that would lead to a more potent force of soldiers being led to the camp just as we were celebrating victory.

No, that wouldn't be good.

We must take the control of the camp as a whole and not let the outside world know it had been done. In order to do that, we could not mess with that electric car. It might be the only contact between the camp and the central government. The last thing we needed was more trouble than that for which we were already planning.

I read on.

"100 victories in 100 battles is not the most skillful. Subduing the other's military without battle is the most skillful."

Up until now we were resigned to the fact that we were going to have to go through hell to liberate the camps. There would be gunfire and there would be bloodshed. But when I thought about it, maybe that wasn't necessarily the case.

I sat down and drew a small map of the camp. We didn't need a whole faction of men to attack from one direction – be it from the fields or the main gate. What we needed was to just make sure that the guys with the guns did not get a chance to shoot them.

There were typically only two men guarding the workers in the fields. They could be easily overcome with two or three men in the truck loaded with weapons, which would immediately arm the field workers, who were also the most capable people in the camp. One or two men could appear at the base of the watch tower as the guards changed shifts, which they typically did in a sloppy fashion – one man coming down, then the other man going up. Once the tower was neutralized the truck and the newly armed field workers could storm the camp from one end, while the rest of the men stormed the camp from the front gates.

When I looked at my new drawing, I knew that Sun Tzu was certainly correct – there was definitely an 'art' to war.

I presented my plan to Mitch and Ed the following day. Mitch immediately became a strong proponent of the strategy, but I knew that would be the case. I was more concerned about Ed. Once I was able to convince him that hijacking the car was not necessarily smart because it might draw undue attention to us, he fell right in line and gave my new plan complete support.

One of our main concerns was that we were still very thin in numbers. The plan looked great on paper, but should the enemy get off a few lucky shots at the outset of the battle, we were going to be short-handed on one of our fronts, and that would make success a lot more questionable.

Mitch and I would take the truck with its bed loaded with weapons, take control of the guards in the fields and distribute the weapons to the field workers. Colin and Junior would solidify the guard in the watch tower as they changed shifts. Ed and the rest of the boys would wait until the field workers had distracted most of the guards' attention, and then assault the main buildings in the front of the camp in the hope that they could get there before any sort of distress signal could be sent out.

To me, this was the most dangerous of the assignments, but Ed seemed to take great pride in the fact that he was leading it. I just hoped he was up to the job and I hoped even more that Pete wouldn't chicken out. Part of me felt as though I should tell Ed that he might have a problem with Pete, but as we handed out the assignments, I stared Pete right in the face as if to challenge him. He looked me coldly in the eyes and nodded, as if to say, "I won't let you down." I hoped to hell that he wouldn't.

During the whole battle, we had one other trump card up our sleeve and that was our sniper. While the assault took shape, Katie would be sitting up in her nest surveying the scene and eyeing any potential targets. She was also responsible for bringing word back to Charlotte and Anna should something go wrong – a job I did not allow her to forget or take lightly.

The intensity among the group heightened as we got closer and closer to the day of reckoning. None of the men had combat experience. Still, we were confident – especially since it didn't look like our adversaries had much experience either and we had the element of surprise on our side. It helped that we were all in good physical shape and armed to the teeth.

As far as we knew, we had all our bases covered and there are only so many times you can practice and run-through a plan without overdoing it. So the morning of the day before the assault, we gathered yet again. The men and Katie were expecting another day of drilling and practice, but I surprised them.

"We are not going to drill today." They looked at me with confusion – even Big Ed Marino. "Today, I want you to take a day for yourself and prepare your mind. Do whatever you need to do knowing that tomorrow will be the most important day of your life. We are all counting on one another, and there are many good people down at that camp, many who are near and dear to us, and they are counting on us as well." I made sure to look at Katie as I said that, to let her know I was thinking about Jimmy, too. "Make peace with your personal decision to do this – sit in your home, collect your thoughts, think about your future. Then come back tomorrow morning. We'll do one last run through and then we'll give 'em hell."

I didn't expect them to hoot and holler, and they didn't. Their reaction was one of quiet confidence, which is exactly what I was hoping. Many of us had only known one another for a week or so, but we were tied together in a way that most people can never comprehend. We were placing our lives in each others' hands. Taking a moment, we shared handshakes and hugs and whatever else guys do to reinforce a sense of camaraderie. Everyone agreed that taking the day off was a good choice, and they jumped on their bikes and headed down the hill.

Anna and Charlotte came out of the house to join me and Mitch on the porch. I had been so focused on planning everything over the past few days that I had somewhat ignored both of them, which was now giving me a distinct feeling of guilt. This day off was as much needed for me as for anyone else.

Running around the back yard with Anna reminded me of how she would skip down the aisles of the library in search of her favorite book, before the library became something dark and empty. I couldn't help but think of the childhood she was going to miss out on – going to school, making friends, playing sports. I always thought that one day she'd be in high school and I'd be sitting in the bleachers watching her play soccer, or lacrosse, or field hockey. Now, I was no longer so sure that would ever happen. The world had changed so quickly and so drastically that it was hard to believe we could ever return to normalcy.

I took a break and watched Charlotte and Anna toss around the football. Anna had gotten so much better at it over the years since the days when she would pretend to return kicks while her Dad watered the garden. Now she was zipping around perfect spirals nearly every time.

Mitch came over and stood next to me while the girls played. "Amazing how far we've come in such a short time," he observed.

"I was just thinking the same thing."

I looked around at what was once a comfortable backyard I could mow on the weekends. It had been expanded, the grass mostly removed and planted over with vegetables – not exactly the scene I had planned when I bought the house. Where it once played a role as an empty area for a child to play, it now represented our lifeline and perhaps the only thing that kept us from reporting to the food camps ourselves.

"I'm gonna take Anna down to the lake," Mitch offered.

"Sounds like a good idea," I concurred. "Let's go."

"No," Mitch chuckled. "I'm going to take her to the lake. You're going to stay here." He nodded over at Charlotte and I then I knew what he meant. There was no need to say it, but this could very well be the last day we'd have together. "Just meet us down by the lake later." He rose up from the chair and jogged over to the girls, intercepting one of Anna's passes to her mother.

"Anna," Mitch called. "Whaddya say we go for a swim down at the lake?"

Charlotte looked up as well, apparently understanding Mitch's attempt to allow us to have some time alone. Whenever given the opportunity to head up to the lake, Anna grew very excited and tore off in that direction.

"I guess I'd better chase after her," Mitch said.

"I guess so."

And away they went, leaving Charlotte and me there alone for the first time in a long time. We held hands in the yard and watched as Anna and Mitch disappeared into the woods. Then, without words, we walked into the house.

The burdens of this new world we lived in seemed to weigh us both down to the point where we no longer even considered being intimate with each other anymore. It wasn't that we didn't love each other – we certainly did. It was that there was always too much else going on – our self-sufficient lifestyle, the new tenants in the house, or homeschooling our child. All of these things were major changes and we were focused on holding the whole thing together and forgot about the importance of spending time alone with each other.

In a way, the fact that it had been so long gave it a renewed sense of freshness. It sort of made it feel as though it was the first time all over again. What made it truly unique was the obvious possibility that it might well be the last time if things were to go wrong tomorrow. I don't know if that thought ever occurred to Charlotte, but it sure did cross my mind and I tried my best to remember each breath, and every touch.

It could have been sad if I let it. But instead, it felt glorious.

"We're going to have to figure out a way to do this more often," I said.

Charlotte agreed and we took a few more moments to enjoy a loving embrace and enjoy the moment.

We left the house the same way we had entered it – holding hands – and we made our way back to the lake to meet up with Mitch and Anna. Before the water even came into view we could hear splashing and the laughing of a little girl just swimming and having fun.

"Wait," Charlotte said, slowly peering around the leaves to catch a glimpse.

Anna was jumping from a make-shift dock that had been there since we moved in, which was really not much more than a long, upside-down wooden box. The two of them were laughing relentlessly as she launched herself into the water another time.

"You know," I said to Charlotte, "Most of the time, I think that we're doing the right thing by going through with this. But then I see her out here having fun – with no TV or video games or public school and I just can't help but think we could live this way. Why were we ever slaves to all that stuff anyway?"

So wrapped up in our own business, we failed to care enough for each other and it left multitudes of people believing their only option was to surrender their lives to government care and control. A century ago, our ancestors would have laughed at today's problems: the need for high-speed internet connections, safety nets for retirees, precision guidance systems for our weaponry, cheap gasoline for our SUV's and sports cars, and social programs that gave away too much without asking for anything in return. Issues like this tore away at our fabric and led to the collapse of the economy.

Our forefathers had never had this problem – if they needed food, they hunted for it, or they grew it. They didn't sit on their ass and say, "Please help me." They helped themselves.

Never was this as evident to me as in that moment. My eight-year -old daughter having the time of her life in what amounted to a large, water-filled hole in the ground. No video games, no television shows, not even any electricity. It was a rare moment of purity.

Why did we ever think we needed to have anything more?

For a moment, I thought about giving up on the assault. How great would it be if every day could be exactly like today? But I knew that there was no going back.

"Let's go," Charlotte suggested.

"Ok."

And with that, I sprinted around the corner and cannon-balled into the lake.

CHAPTER TWENTY-ONE

It was very difficult to sleep that night. The anticipation of the next day's events was something I had never experienced before. On any given day there is some chance that you might not make it to the next, but it felt as though the odds for me tomorrow were a little bit longer than usual.

I trusted our plan. We had gone over multiple scenarios and many angles of attack, eventually settling on what we thought was the best course of action. After practicing it so often the past few days, it gave me a great sense of confidence, nearly to the point of comfort. Yet I still couldn't get the butterflies out of my stomach. The chances were likely that shots would be fired, which meant that no matter how much we practiced, somebody might go down. I wasn't sure that any of us were prepared for that.

The recurring thought of Pete freezing at gunpoint made me wonder what might happen if more of the guys buckled. Maybe I should have drilled them harder on experiencing that type of pressure. It was too late now.

Charlotte looked fast asleep, but I knew there was no way that I was going to be able to join her. So, I decided to get up and head to the window where Mitch was keeping watch. There was no need for us to change our routine, so we still kept watch even on the last night.

"Hey," I said lightly, trying not to startle him.

"What's up?" he said, perking up in his chair.

"Can't sleep."

"I wonder why," Mitch joked.

I sat in the chair next to him and we both looked out the window, while continuing to speak to one another. Neither of us had ever been trained in taking a watch, but by now we were pretty good at keeping one eye on the task while carrying on a conversation.

"I don't know what I'm worried about. They're never going to know what hit 'em."

"I think you're right," Mitch agreed, cautious not to seem too overconfident. "I think they are so overwhelmed with keeping the camp in line and they seem undertrained to handle what is about to be unleashed on them."

I nodded in agreement. The nod was sincere – it was exactly the way I felt, complete with a sense of concern over my overconfidence.

"You know," Mitch said, "you don't have to go through with this."

"What?" I asked in surprise that he would even think of saying something like that.

He took a deep breath before explaining, making sure his words came out the right way. "You have a family, Ray – Charlotte and Anna. You're the only one with a young child in the group. Ed's kids are all grown and of their own mind. Anna needs you and the price of mission failure is steeper for you than for anyone else."

Those were certainly my fears, too, but I always felt selfish thinking that my life was somehow more important than the others.

"There's still time to change the plan," Mitch said. "Colin can come in the truck with me and Junior can handle the watchtower. I never thought we needed two men on that job anyway."

Over the past few weeks I had held up such a front of confidence and toughness that I never had much time to contemplate my own position. Of course, Mitch's suggestion was out of the question, but his concern was that of a good friend and it was something that, in the moment, actually made me feel better about the whole situation.

"Thanks for the offer, Mitch," I said. "You've been a great friend through this, but you know I'm going to be right next to you in that truck tomorrow. I wouldn't have it any other way." Something gave me the feeling that, after our little chat, I might finally be able to get some sleep. It would only be a few hours before it was my turn to keep watch, but I figured a little sleep would be better than none.

I got up from the chair and began to leave the room before

something unexpected stopped me from heading to bed at that moment. It was a loud knock at the front door.

Mitch and I quickly turned to one another. "Did you see anything?" I asked.

"No."

"Shit."

I grabbed a pistol and Mitch took a shotgun. We quickly made our way down the stairs to the front door. As we got to the bottom the knock repeated, proving there was no chance that the first one was just the wind, or maybe a wandering bear.

Mitch stood in the hall next to the stairs as I walked to the door. It was very reminiscent of an incident just about a month before when we opened the door to greet Art Brady. I grabbed the knob, twisted it and opened. Two men, dressed completely in black stood on the front porch, large guns draped over their shoulders. The one standing closest to me lifted his head, revealing a face that bore a familiar crescent-shaped scar on his right cheek.

"I'm not sure we've really formally met," he said in a familiar raspy tone. "Name is Hank. Hank Masterson." He held out his hand and I shook it as I introduced myself.

"Ray... Ray Stanton," I said.

For a relatively thin man, he had a noticeably tight grip. He then fished into his pocket, and when his hand emerged, he held it out towards me revealing the ring I had given him a few days prior. After recognizing it, I looked back up at him. He nodded – an unspoken consent to take the ring from his hand, which I did and then placed it back on the finger where it belonged.

"Thank you," I said, taking an extra long look before remembering there was a second leg of this transaction. "Give me one minute and I'll get something to replace it."

As I turned to head back inside, he interrupted. "That won't be necessary." I hesitated and looked back a little confused. "As long as you still got those bullets."

"You mean you want them back?" I asked, not quite understanding what he meant.

"No," he said. "I meant as long as you haven't used them. Have you attacked the camp yet?"

"No," I answered. "Tomorrow."

"Good," he said. Then, alternately pointing his thumb at himself and then his compatriot he said, "We're in."

I shook my head in a confused sort of manner. "What? You're what?"

"We're in," he confirmed. "If you can use us, of course."

I wasn't about to turn down assistance – especially from someone who was clearly much better trained than us. "Of course we can use you. Come on in."

Hank introduced us to his younger brother, a very quiet but skilled soldier named Steven whom I had met once before – the man in the rafters. I introduced them to Mitch, who had lowered his shotgun but still carried it with him. I still had the pistol tucked in my belt, but I knew it wouldn't matter at this point. The guns these men carried were not recreational, but they no longer intimidated me. Instead, I was happy they were part of our arsenal.

We went into the office, where I lit the candles creating a dimly lit ambiance. A mock-up map of the camp still hung on the wall.

"This the camp?" Hank asked.

"Yeah," I acknowledged.

"May I?" he asked.

"Of course."

He walked over to map and stared at it – the various features, pawns and lines I had learned how to draw from my library studies. "Pretty good," he said, sounding somewhat impressed.

I moved over to the map and explained the plan from soup-to-nuts, being as detailed as I possibly could. I knew that Hank had been militarily trained and for as much as I had studied, it helped ease my mind to have someone qualified to look over my shoulder and say, "Yes, that's a good job."

I pointed and explained, pointed some more and explained some more, and finally, when I was finished, Hank spoke up. "Yes," he said. "That's a good job."

I felt a rushing sense of vindication resulting from his approval.

"But," he said, and the sense of approval quickly vanished, "there are some problems here."

I exhaled, a little concerned that I hadn't thought of everything. "Well," I sighed. "It's my first battle plan."

Everyone chuckled.

"And it's a good one," he assured me. "But I have one concern. How do you know that as soon as they hear you coming, they won't call for back-up and send soldiers to come and wipe you out while you're celebrating?"

"It's a concern of mine, for sure," I explained. "But we're going to get to those buildings as quick as we possibly can."

"Cut the lines," he said.

"What?"

"Cut the lines. Or at least temporarily disable them and then put them back together."

"Nobody in our crew knows how to do that," I said.

"We do," Hank said.

With that, Hank picked up a marker from the desk and hit the map. "Steven and I will leave shortly and head to the camp. We'll meet you guys there. When dawn comes, we'll be able to assess the situation. Once we cut the electric and the phones, we'll join up with this group here, led by???"

"Ed Marino," I answered.

"No shit," he said. "Me and Ed go way back."

I wasn't surprised. Liberty Gulch was a pretty small town.

"We'll get in there quick and keep them from calling for back-up. Then, once it's secure, we'll head back up and re-connect the power. It'll be quick – hopefully quick enough so as not to draw attention. And it doesn't mess up any other part of your plan."

"Okay," I agreed. "Deal."

"One other question," he said.

"What's that?"

"Where is that pussy you were with at my house? Where's he going to be?"

"Pete?" I asked, identifying the culprit by name. "He's with you," I said.

"Okay," he said in a defeatist tone as if he had just doubled-down on an "11" and drew a deuce. "I'll handle it."

"I spoke with him," I added. "I think he'll be ok."

"We'll see."

With that, the men packed up and left. They hadn't been there for long, but everything had changed. I just hoped it was in a good way. The house was quiet again, and it was getting late.

"Do you think that was a good idea?" Mitch asked.

"They have experience and they have weapons. Those machine guns give us a distinct advantage."

"I agree," Mitch said. "Hell, they were able to sneak up on us. We didn't even see them coming."

I looked at the clock. It was 2 in the morning. "Shit, it's late," I said.

"You tired *now?*" Mitch asked.

"Actually, I am," I answered. "The hell with the last watch. We both need our rest."

Mitch agreed, and we retired to our rooms. Taking my normal place next to Charlotte, I draped my arm around her, silently giving her a kiss on the cheek. And then, I slept.

CHAPTER TWENTY-TWO

At first daylight we awoke to another loud knock at the front door along with a bit of lively commotion. All of the men showed up at the same time anxious to begin the day, although it had less to do with the impending battle than it did with the eggs and bacon Ed Marino brought with him.

"Slaughtered a pig yesterday," he said, holding aloft a large slab of meat. "Thought we could all use a nice breakfast before we headed out this morning."

"I'll take that," answered Charlotte, grabbing the bacon and heading into the kitchen. Junior handed over a large basket of eggs, which I gladly accepted as everyone filed into the house. If anything, the mood was cautiously jovial – the impending full country breakfast was something most of us hadn't had in quite a while and was enough to lift our mood above the danger of today's planned assault.

Everyone milled about the living room chatting and joking with one another. I couldn't help but feel proud of how we had all come together. I may have smiled and joked right alongside them had there not been something specific on my mind that I needed to address.

"Ed, you have a moment?" I asked as I walked into the kitchen to help Charlotte with the food. "Here, let me take that," I said to Charlotte, and grabbed the knife from her. As I started cutting nice, thick slices of bacon, Ed appeared behind me.

"What's on your mind?" he asked.

"Ever hear of a guy named Hank Masterson?"

His eyes widened at hearing the name. "Yeah," he began. "Real tough kid. Joined the Marine Corps and I think he spent some time in Iraq – the first war, not the latest one." He hesitated for a moment, as if trying to awaken his memory. "I used to see him around all the time, but not in years. I'm not sure whatever happened to him."

"Well, you know the guy that got us the bullets for your daughter's gun?"

"Yeah."

"Same guy."

"No shit," Ed calmly responded at this information. He may have sensed some frustration emanating from me, and truth be told there may have been some. After all, perhaps it wouldn't have been necessary for me to be held at gunpoint in Hank's driveway if Ed had put two-and-two together. "Not sure I would have ever guessed that."

I wasn't blaming him, though, and I just wanted to move on to what was more important. "That's not a problem, Ed. I wouldn't have expected you to know that. What I really want to know is: do you think we can trust him?"

"Trust him?" Ed thought for a moment. "Trust him how?"

I quickly recapped the prior night.

"Hank and his brother Steven came to the house last night with automatic weapons," I explained. "I had told them about the raid we were planning and they wanted to help us. Right now, as we speak, they are down at the camp analyzing how to take down the camp's communications network before we storm in. Then, they plan to join your group in the assault. So, can we trust them?"

Ed thought for a long moment, before responding plainly. "Yes," he stated confidently. "Yes, I think we can trust him."

His point-blank answer alleviated much of my concern over whether or not it was a good idea to bring Hank and Steven into the fold so late in the game. If there was one thing I knew about Ed, it was that he was a careful evaluator of character. If Ed trusted the guy, then so could I.

"Good," I answered.

"But," Ed interrupted, "is he going to be in charge of our leg of the assault or will that job remain with me?"

So concerned with the trustworthiness of our new companions, I hadn't even thought about how their addition might affect Ed's leadership role. Perhaps more importantly, by asking this question Ed had somewhat subordinated himself to me, which was surprising. I had never once asked for this role, but now it seemed I officially had it. The men listened to me. All of them, even Ed Marino. I never asked for the role, but it appeared to have landed squarely on my lap. Who knew that when Art Brady pushed his way through my front door just a few weeks ago, it would lead to my becoming the leader of a revolution?

Despite this, being a pushy leader was not my style. My style was more straight-forward honesty and empowerment, and I was not about to risk disrupting the group by demoting its senior member the day of the assault.

"I hadn't thought of that, Ed. But that is your decision. It seemed to me as though these men were very well trained and that is what we having been lacking the most. But if you're uncomfortable with that, I will back you."

"No," Ed chimed in. "I'm not uncomfortable with that. Hank is a trained soldier, and I'm just a farmer. He is more capable of leading the assault."

I was shocked at how quickly Ed let loose the reins of control, but I figured on the morning of your first military assault, one might be a little more nervous than normal.

"Ed, you're a good man," I proclaimed, "and you're an important part of this mission. I need you on board with every facet of our plan. Are we good?"

"We're good."

"Then I have one more bit of news," I said. "Since you have two new members on your assault team, Mitch and I will be taking Pete along with us. Is that a deal?"

"It's a deal."

It was a decision I made on the fly, but it seemed like a fair one. Mitch and I could use an extra hand taking control of the field – it was already difficult enough that one of us had to drive the truck and hold a gun at the same time. We were now adding two experienced soldiers with automatic weapons on the assault team that would take the main building. Plus, for some strange reason I had confidence that Pete wouldn't let me down. Hank had gone out of his way to mention Pete's presence on the assault team and I knew he wouldn't have that confidence in him after seeing Pete in action that day in his driveway. I could put Pete behind the wheel of the truck where I felt I could trust him, and then Hank wouldn't have to look over his shoulder to monitor what he clearly felt was a weak link.

As Ed left the kitchen, I couldn't help but think how perfectly the pieces had fallen into place. I confirmed my instincts regarding Hank and Steven; we substituted a more qualified leader into what was perhaps the most difficult and dangerous part of the mission, and added a member to my own squad where I really thought he could be more effective

I finished cutting the bacon as Charlotte began preparing the eggs. There was no easy way to cook these days – we typically either used the barbeque grill outside, or a large pot we rigged over the fireplace.

The soldiers were all in the living room, and I could hear a faint sound of music in the distance. It sounded a bit like a guitar playing... my guitar?

"One of the boys must know how to play," I noted to Charlotte.

"Maybe you should go check it out," she said. I looked down at the food and the task that awaited us. "Don't worry. I got this," Charlotte said.

Making my way towards the living room, the music got louder and louder and I could make out a girl's voice singing the words to Pearl Jam's *"Elderly Woman Behind the Counter in a Small Town,"* one of my all-time favorites. All was quiet except for one solitary voice; one beautiful voice producing the lyrics with which I was so familiar, having played the song almost every night for my family over the last few months.

When I turned the corner, there was my little girl sitting in a chair strumming away at her daddy's guitar and singing with a voice as lovely as her mother's. At some point I caught her eye and she smiled at me, piercing my heart with pride. A moment later, Charlotte's hand tapped my shoulder.

"When did she learn the guitar?" I asked her.

"She took a book out of the library and has been working at it for months while you were outside working in the yard. She wanted to surprise you."

"I'm surprised," I admitted. Learning to play guitar wasn't something you just did overnight. It took a lot of practice. "What an amazing surprise."

"Me, you wouldn't recall," she sang, "for I'm not my farmer."

There were a couple of muffled giggles from the boys who knew the word was "former" and not "farmer." I could certainly understand the slip-up since she hadn't had access to the lyrics and had learned the song only by memorizing her mother and father singing it in the months after the power had gone out.

When she finished the last verse and rang the last chord, the room erupted in applause. Anna blushed in embarrassment before getting up from the chair and running over to me and giving me a huge hug. The prideful tears welling in my eyes reached maximum capacity before succumbing to the volume limits, and one lonely tear streamed down my cheek.

"I wanted to learn to play guitar like you, Daddy."

"You did great, sweetie. You did great."

The men, and Katie, enjoyed a great breakfast and once the morning began to push towards noon, we knew it was time to get moving. The truck was loaded with the weapons we would distribute to the field laborers, and there was the bicycle for Katie to race home on in case things went badly.

Hugging Charlotte good-bye, I tried not to wonder if that might be the last time I did so. She must have sensed my trepidation.

"Don't even think that way," she whispered. "We'll see you tonight when you get back." With that, we exchanged a kiss that was more of a "see you later" than a "hopelessly romantic good-bye forever."

Lastly, Anna ran up and gripped her dad tightly. She knew what was going on, but we had tried hard to play down the danger involved. I am pretty sure she saw through that as she lassoed me around the neck tighter than ever before.

"I love you, Daddy," she said.

"I love you too."

"Be home for dinner," she said.

"I'll try, sweetie. Maybe we can work on some new songs."

"Ok, Dad."

With that, I kissed her forehead and lowered her back down to the ground. I got behind the wheel with Mitch, Colin, Katie and Ed in the cab, while everyone else piled into the truck bed. It was a little crowded, but the truck was big enough to handle it.

Every drop of gasoline we had left was in that truck, but the meter was still pretty low. I knew we'd get there and have plenty for the assault, but I wasn't 100% sure we'd make it back. Of course, that would be more than a welcome problem.

I coasted down the hill in neutral and after a few minutes we found ourselves heading through what were once the thriving malls of Liberty Gulch. These days it looked more like a ghost town. I put the truck in gear and we headed towards the camp. The ride was very quiet – I hoped it wasn't because people were nervous, but rather because they were focusing on the job they had ahead of them. I know I was.

The ride was uneventful and, as usual, we saw not a soul on our way to the back entrance to the hill where we had spied on the camps. In recent days, we had built a small spot to hide the truck and I pulled right in.

As we exited the truck with the assault teams and our sniper readying their weapons, Hank and Steven found us and came over.

"How'd you find us so quickly?" I asked.

"That truck," Hank said. "I could hear you coming from a mile away. You're going to have to be careful driving that thing." He looked at the vehicle, now in its hiding spot, and nodded in approval at its camouflage before adding, "We better move out now, just in case they heard you, too."

"All right, everyone," I said. "Let's move out."

"Hey, Hank," Ed Marino greeted our newest member.

"Ed," Hank said with a nod. "You sure you're up for this?" he asked.

"You sure you are?" Ed kidded lightheartedly.

"Let's cut this reunion short and hustle up," I interjected. "If Hank and Steve were able to hear the truck coming, then maybe the guards could hear it, too. I don't want to lose our element of surprise before we even get started."

We hiked up the hill about 10 minutes to where a natural clearing in the woods allowed us enough space to congregate. Hank and Steven were armed with their assault weapons, while the rest of the men carried the most advanced weaponry in our stash, other than Katie's sniper rifle, of course.

Mitch, Pete, and I stood there watching as everyone else sat in a circle, checking their weapons one last time. It was about an hour and a half until the assault would begin and I wanted to go through one final walkthrough before we separated. You could sense the tension in the air – with the exception of Hank, these weren't soldiers. They were ordinary citizens. Never could they have expected to find themselves in this position – a few hours away from glory, or a bullet away from death.

Only Hank looked confident and stoic in his stature and I could tell his attitude and confidence were already rubbing off a little bit on the team. So, what better place to start the discussion than with him.

"Ok, let's go over this one more time," I began. "Hank, what were you able to find?"

He answered dutifully, as a soldier would to a superior. "Sir, Steven and I found the electric feed. The wires can be cut from a fairly safe distance."

"Ok," I said. "Mitch, Pete and I will wait until the watchtower guard is being relieved and then drive the truck right through the field. We will subdue the two guards at gunpoint and distribute the weapons to the field workers before joining the rest of you at the main camp.

"Once you hear that truck engine fire up, cut the wires. Which one of you was planning on doing the cutting?"

"That's your call, sir," Hank answered.

"Which one of you is more skilled?" I asked.

"I am," Steven offered.

I looked quizzically at Hank and he nodded in affirmation.

"Good," I said. "Perfect. Steven, you will cut the wire using the roar of the truck engine as your cue. Hank, you will be leading the assault team."

There was a collective gasp from the men, since I had forgotten to alert them to this last minute change.

"Sir?" Hank acknowledged. "I thought Ed Marino would be leading the team, sir."

"Yes, he was," I affirmed. "But we think with your experience that you would be most effective in that role."

Ed Marino stood up and reinforced my statement. "Hank, I've known you for a long time. I may not have seen you for years, but I remember you as a good, smart man and I know you have the experience to lead us. It is my honor to serve under you... Sir."

The tension among the team immediately eased.

"I am honored," Hank said with a nod.

The discipline, graciousness and professionalism of the men in front of me were remarkable. I had felt it all along, but at this moment the pride I felt to be with them was palpable.

"You can go over any details and particulars once we're through," I said. "But for now, let's continue going over the plan.

"Steven will cut the wires and then join the assault team as quickly as possible. Colin and Junior – your cue will be the same. Wait for the guards to change and then when you hear the truck's engine race across that field, get out there and stop those guards from taking a position in the tower. Got it?"

"Yes, sir," they both responded in unison, continuing our sudden transformation from ragtag militia to disciplined military assault team.

"The assault team will then move in through the gates, with the ultimate goal of taking control of the main building before they have a chance to restore power or radio for help. Katie?"

"Yes, sir," came a confident voice from the back in a female tone.

"Set yourself up in the perch," I said. "Keep your eye open for targets. You know how the plan is supposed to shake out – do your best to anticipate trouble and help out if you can."

"Yes, sir."

"And Katie," I added hesitantly, not wanting to seem as though I was jinxing the mission. "You know what you need to do if…" I couldn't finish, but the message got through. I was talking about her bike ride back home should things go wrong.

"Yes, sir," she said. "I know."

I shared a look with Ed Marino, who nodded in approval at the mention. If things went horribly wrong, it would be our women – Charlotte, Anna and Katie – who would have to make do without us.

My recap seemed to go by rather quickly and I had a sense I couldn't just leave it there.

"Gentlemen," I said in somewhat of a preacher's tone, with any movement among them ceasing and all noise silenced. "And Katie," I added with a little smile which drew a little laugh from the men. "What we are about to do is the most important thing any of us has ever done in our lives. What we are doing is of a historical nature. They may very well write books or make movies about today.

"The best part is that we are definitively on the side of good. We are here to liberate our friends and neighbors, who arrived months ago at this camp under the promise that they would be fed, they would be safe, and things would eventually return to normal. But things have gotten worse for them and now they are being imprisoned and forced to work hard labor in these fields.

"We will strike fast, exactly as we have practiced. We will succeed."

They all nodded in approval. I looked over at Hank, who took over from there barking out orders as to how he envisioned his leg of the assault. He exuded confidence and it didn't hurt that his automatic rifle was slung over his shoulder. Looking at him and then looking out at our adversaries, the guards in the camp, I knew we had the upper hand. Hank was a soldier. He had done this before. Those men down there were amateurs.

We finally saw the electric car leave the compound on schedule, and the three of us left the group and walked back down the hill to the truck. With each step closer, the realization of the moment began to find the pit of my stomach. A few weeks ago, I wasn't convinced we would actually be going through with this. But now here it was – the time was approaching fast. The people I left in those woods would be counting on me and I wasn't about to let them down.

"Pete," I said.

"Yes, sir," he answered, a quiver of uncertainty in his voice.

"You know how to drive?" I asked.

"Yes, sir."

"Good. Because you're going behind the wheel on this mission while Mitch and I ride in back."

A feeling of relief emanated from both men. Pete certainly seemed happy that he wouldn't be holding a gun, and Mitch seemed to be happy to have his long-time, trusted friend literally standing by his side during the most frightening moment of our lives.

Pete snagged the key out of midair when I tossed it to him.

"Thank you, sir," he said.

"Don't let me down."

"Never, sir," he pledged. I could sense that Pete had a great deal of respect for me. I never told his friends about the way he buckled at gunpoint when we went to get Katie's ammunition, and I'm fairly certain he was thankful for that. Now I was putting him in an important role that was perfect for his demeanor, and he was thankful. I had confidence in his words – he wasn't going to let me down.

Uncovering the truck from its hiding spot, the three of us entered the cab with Pete in the driver's seat, me in the passenger side and Mitch in the back. Pete put the key in the ignition and started her up. Taking a deep breath, he put it into gear and hit the accelerator.

"Not too hard," I advised. "Remember what Hank said about the noise."

"Yes, sir," he said.

We slowly drove around the compound towards the spot we chose as a waiting area. Even though we were driving slowly, it didn't take very long to get there and now we were really ready for the show to begin.

"Ok," I said when I first eyed the spot. "Cut it, and then ease it into that spot over there."

There was a small raised berm between the road and the field and the truck fit nicely behind it. About a quarter mile before reaching it, Pete threw the car into neutral and cut the ignition. We coasted slowly the rest of the way, barely maintaining enough speed to come to rest behind the berm.

Mitch opened the window between the truck's cab and the bed and the two of us got out, leaving Pete behind the wheel. I walked over to the driver's side and Pete rolled down the window.

"Here," I said, handing him the handgun I had been carrying. "You might need this in an emergency."

"Thanks," he said, taking it from my hand. "...sir", he added after a delay, as if he forgot that I suddenly outranked him in our informal army.

I smiled. "You're gonna do fine."

Climbing into the truck bed where Mitch had already peeled back the canvas that hid our cache, I picked up the semi-automatic rifle I was going to use, or hopefully not use but rather just point in a threatening manner. Mitch painted his face with some eye-black he had found in a box of old baseball equipment from the basement. I looked at him, and chuckled.

"Want some?" he asked.

"No thanks."

"I look more menacing this way," he said to my amusement. He was right, though – it did make him look more menacing. Since surprise and intimidation were major facets of our plan, I couldn't laugh at him for too long. It made a lot of sense and for a second I thought about painting myself, but I just didn't think we should all look like violent soldiers out there. Someone needed to reflect a human side and perhaps some of the captives would even recognize my face and that could help put them at ease.

"Have you taken a look yet?" I asked, nodding towards the small hill, over which were the fields we were to assault.

"No," he said.

"What are we waiting for?" I asked, and handed him the set of binoculars.

Using the cab to help him balance, he stepped on the side of the pick-up and peered over the berm.

"Oh shit," he said almost under his breath before quickly dropping back into the truckbed.

"What? What? What?" I asked.

"They're right there!" he said in a hushed voice.

"Who? Who?"

"The guards," he hushed. Pete turned and looked at us through the window. "The guards are about 20 feet behind this hill and all the workers are just beyond them in the field.

"Ok, ok," I said. "Let me take a look. Clearly, if they knew we were here, we would know by now. So let's just all be quiet and chill out."

I slowly lifted myself on the side-rail of the truck and peered over the berm. Mitch was right – the guards were right there, backs toward us, rifles in hand, standing next to each other chatting away.

I knelt back into the truck bed. Another stroke of good luck. Had Hank not warned me of the noise the truck engine made, I might have just pulled it right into the spot. But being aware of that fact and sneaking into the notch behind the berm with the engines off had appeared to keep us from being detected.

"This is good news, fellas," I advised in a hushed tone. "Slight change of plan. Mitch and I are going on that berm. Pete, you fire up the truck and take it into the field. Once you get around the corner, lay off the gas for a second so they'll hear us when we tell them to drop their weapons. When you see us crest the berm, count to 'two one-thousand' and gun it again to get those weapons to the workers. It will be quick. Then we'll all hop in and get our ass over to help out with the assault team. Got it?"

I didn't know if the fact that I could come up with a small change of plan like that on the fly was because of all the book-reading I had done on battle-tactics, or if it was just something that came to me naturally. Mitch and Pete both nodded confidently and gave a hushed and unnecessary, "Yes, sir."

"As long as they are unaware of our presence beforehand," I continued whispering, "this will make things a lot easier for us. Let's just avoid being detected until those guards in the watch tower change their post. And then, we're off."

Mitch and I quietly snuck out of the truck bed along with our weapons. We crawled up the berm, staying as low as we possibly could. As we got to the top, I whispered, "You keep an eye on the guards. If they see us, you let me know – we'll have to go early. I'll use the binoculars on those watchtowers and wait for them to change."

Mitch nodded. A "Yes, sir" was clearly not warranted since we were now so close to the enemy and didn't want to be heard.

I was very concerned about the man in that tower. If we were seen and then forced to move early, there was no way to let the other assault teams know. The watchtower would be manned and alert.

Reaching the top of the hill, I peeked ever so slowly over the edge with the binoculars. I could get a pretty good look at the tower without seeing the nearby guards in the field, so it felt pretty safe. Now that we were so close to the top of the berm, I could hear the scritch-scratching of the field worker's tools as they went about their daily work. If I listened intently, I could hear the guards' voices in mumbled tones, though I was unable to make out anything they were saying. It didn't really matter, because my focus was entirely on that tower.

A guard armed with a rifle paced back and forth in the tower. I wasn't sure if that was how they train lookouts, or if he was just bored shitless standing up there all alone for hours. I checked my watch. It wouldn't be long now; the guards typically changed on the hour.

"Get ready, Mitch," I whispered. "We're getting close."

Sitting there contemplating the possibilities of what might happen in the next few moments put even more butterflies in my stomach. This was going to happen and I just had to let the training take over and do it. There was no holding back. I finally saw the replacement guard heading toward the tower. With every step he took, our moment grew closer and closer. I just hoped that the rest of the assault team could see what I was seeing and were ready to go.

As the replacement guard got close to the base of the watchtower, the one up top neared the ladder and began to descend. When he neared the half-way point, I could practically count the remaining steps. One step after the other, it was like a ticking clock winding down until mayhem broke loose.

Three, two, one, his foot hit the dirt and I turned to Pete, who was attentively waiting my instruction.

"NOW! NOW!"

CHAPTER TWENTY-THREE

Pete turned the ignition and the truck's engine roared to life. In an instant, he had it in drive and barreled around the berm.

Mitch and I raced over the hill, guns drawn and "mean-faces" on. The engines on the truck hesitated, just as planned, giving me my moment to yell, "Drop your weapons! Hands in the air!"

The guards were completely taken by surprise and put up no fight whatsoever. Dropping their guns in unison, both of them reached their hands for the sky.

"Hit the ground!" I said, with Pete now racing the truck towards the field workers. As I pointed the gun at our new prisoners, Mitch tied their hands behind their backs with twine. We had no way of knowing if the rest of the team was now going about their business – if the watchtower guards had been as easy to subdue as the ones in the field, or if Steven had properly cut the phones and the electricity. We had to trust them and focus on our job.

All of the field workers headed for the truck to arm themselves where Pete had stopped and begun to disperse the weaponry. All of them except one – one worker headed over to us as we tied up the guards.

"Foggdog!" I said. I never thought I'd be so happy to see him.

"What took you guys so long?" he asked. "I've been here two fucking weeks!"

In the middle of our assault, I could do nothing but laugh. I gave him a quick hug as Mitch continued to tie up the second guard. We picked them both up and dragged them over to the back of the truck, where there now stood a dozen men – mostly slim in stature and dirty from days of hard labor and sweat without showers – but now armed and about to turn their captors into their captives.

We loaded up the truck. As Mitch and I lifted the first of the guards into the truckbed, one of the field workers decided it was time to exact some revenge for the season of forced labor. He pointed the gun at the guard, eliciting a lot of protestation from the group.

"No, no, no!"

But instead of shooting the guard, the man angrily forced the butt-end of the rifle into the guard's chin.

"Hey, hey, hey!" I angrily contested, pulling myself up into the truck and placing myself between the guard and the man who slugged him. Grabbing the man by the collar, I lifted him a few inches into the air. "We have risked our lives to come here and rescue you. There is an assault on the rest of the guards in the camp as we speak and we will be joining that assault momentarily. One thing I will not stand for is anyone reducing themselves to the level of their guards. We will not injure them, we will not touch them. We will respect them as we would any man."

Everyone in the truck bed went silent, as if they were obedient children taking orders from a headmaster.

"Is that understood?" I asked.

There was no answer.

"I will cut off these restraints and give these men their rifles back if you do not answer me. Is that understood?"

In as much unison as a dozen beaten-down men can possibly muster, they all answered, "Yes, sir!"

"Good."

Once we were all in the truck, I made my way to the window and told Pete to head toward the camp. I wasn't quite sure, but I swear when he took his orders, Pete was smiling. I think amidst our early success, he was enjoying his vindication.

The truck's engines roared as we started making our way through the fields towards the camp. The terrain was rough and bumpy and the ride in the truck's bed was anything but comfortable. I tried to survey the scene to figure out where we should go. There were a lot of people mulling about and everything seemed predictably frenzied. I took this as a good sign. If we were losing, people would be hiding out.

"Have you heard any shots?" I asked Mitch and Foggdog, who both stood next to me. They shook their heads. It left a lot of questions unanswered, but it made me cautiously optimistic. Our leg of the battle turned out to be much, much easier than we had ever thought. Now we were depending on our friends to follow through on their end, and we were desperate for confirmation of their success.

With the barracks and tents in our way, I couldn't see what was going on at the base of the watchtower. There was nobody up there, though, confirming to me that Colin and Junior had accomplished their mission and held off the tower guards. That left one more front of the assault – the main building.

From our angle, the main building looked pretty quiet, though I certainly knew that could not be the case. I assumed the electricity was out, but since it was daytime there was no way for me to know for sure. None of the lights had been on in the first place, so I had no idea if they had gone out.

As we drew closer and closer at a slow pace due to the rough terrain, I noticed a funny thing. There was a garage door on the field-side of the main building that we hadn't really noticed before. And the only reason I noticed it now was because it had just opened. A couple of men then appeared, working frantically on some sort of apparatus.

Still, we had heard no shots, but the truck's engine was working so hard that I wasn't convinced we would hear shots even if they were actually being fired. We kept on driving. The armed field workers all seemed ready to do their part in the battle. But for now my eyes were focused on that garage door.

It was only a moment before I realized what it was they were doing. They were wheeling out a generator and getting ready to start it up and send a jolt of electricity through the building to whatever computers and communication devices they had inside.

"Oh shit!" I said.

"What?" asked Mitch.

"They're gonna fire up that generator and then they'll be able to send out a distress signal. Before we know it, there will be military here and we'll all be fucked."

The look on Mitch's face seemed to share my concern and I knew I was right to be worried.

"Pete," I called. "Head for the main building."

"Yes, sir," he said and veered the truck slightly to the right.

We were still a great distance from the building, but I knew from having a gas generator myself that they weren't always easy to get started right away. My attention was solely on the generator now – I still had no idea what was going on in the camp, but I knew that Hank and his team wouldn't be able to see what was going on in the garage from their entrance point. I was hoping they were getting ready to penetrate the main building and prevent anyone from sending out that distress signal, but I had no time to rest my confidence on hope alone. We were going to stop these guys from starting that damn generator. We had to.

The truck continued to barrel ahead, bobbing up and down through the field. We were getting closer, but there was no way any of us could take an accurate shot at the men in the garage. Reaching into my coat pocket, I removed one of the grenades we had recovered from Colin's uncle's house. I stared at it, thinking I would have a better chance to stop them from starting the generator if I threw the grenade rather than take a shot with a rifle from the bed of a pick-up truck being driven on bumpy terrain.

I could see one of the men pouring the gasoline while the other monitored their surroundings as if they knew they had to move quickly. There was no way we were going to make it; no way we could stop them from starting up that generator. All I could think about was that this great plan that took us weeks to hash out was going to go for naught. Everything was going to go perfectly, except we would be forced to leave the camp immediately and lose the whole farm.

I eyed the grenade in my hand and tried to gauge how close we would have to be for me to give it a toss. It reminded me of all the times I had thrown the football in the backyard with Anna and how she used to love to see how far Daddy could throw, even though she dared not attempt to catch the ball at such a distance. I looked back up and knew it was still no good. I wasn't going to be able to reach.

We kept getting closer and I could see the men at the door pulling the ripcord to start the generator. From our distance, I couldn't hear whether or not the generator started, but the men's reaction seemed to corroborate the fact that it had – they simply walked away.

"Fuck, fuck, fuck!" I cursed, imagining that inside that building they were preparing to call for back-up because insurgents were attacking the farm.

And then the first and only shot of the battle rang out.

It was loud as hell, audible even over the roar of the truck's engine. In retrospect, I'm not sure whether the sound I heard was the sound of the gun being fired or the sound of the generator's gasoline tank exploding. It could very well have been the latter.

"What the hell was that?" asked Foggdog.

I thought for a moment before realizing what had actually happened. "I think that was *your girlfriend*," I answered.

"What?"

I was certain that I was right. Watching from her perch up in the woods, Katie had found a worthy target – the generator – and blew it up with surgical precision using her sniper rifle.

"I'll tell you later," I hollered and the truck continued on.

We bounded through the field and into the camp, which was now full of people milling about. I didn't see any of our team, but made way for the garage door, which was still wide open.

The truck stopped and a group of armed field workers piled out.

"How do I work this thing?" asked Foggdog, referring to his rifle.

"Just point it and pull the trigger, dumbass."

Once we were all out on the ground, it seemed again like nobody quite knew what to do, and they looked to me for guidance.

"Foggdog, you keep your eye on the prisoners," I commanded.

He nodded. It was almost refreshing not to hear someone yell, "Yes, sir."

"Everyone else, follow me." We headed through the garage and reached the door that led to the back entrance of the main building. I had no idea what we were going to find on the other side, but at that point we were so close to victory that I just felt the urge to open it and find out.

I turned the knob and thrust my shoulder into the door.

Rushing in, I found myself right in the middle of a big, dimly lit room with what appeared to be a control center in the middle. The monitors were all blackened, a sure sign that the electric was, indeed, down. There was virtually no reaction to our entrance. Instead, all I saw was Hank and Steven with their guns leveled at a group of guards who were sitting up against the farthest wall. Behind Hank and Steven stood the rest of the crew – the Marinos, their friends and

Colin.

"What took you so long?" Hank asked.

Only one thought went through my head at that moment. "Holy shit," I said. "We did it."

At my declaration, a great whooping celebration rang out in the hall. The guards were all subdued and the control room had been taken. I turned around and looked at the field workers who had just come off my truck and, to a man, tears streamed down their cheeks.

I looked around and saw Ed Marino, looking all the part of a soldier standing just behind Hank.

"Hey, Ed," I called. He turned to face me. "Jimmy's outside with a couple more prisoners. Why don't you go invite them inside."

"Yes, sir," he said, his face beaming.

"Steven," I called next.

"Yes, sir," he responded.

"Go repair the lines."

Another, "Yes, sir" rang out, and Steven ran out to do his job.

I turned around and faced the armed men that had just ridden in the back of my truck through the fields. "Gentlemen," I said. "Please go back to your families and tell everyone that the guards have been detained, and you have been rescued."

A look of shock seemed to befall the group, and they just stood there for a moment as if not knowing what it felt like to be a free man again.

"Sir?" one man asked.

"Yes," I said, and the room quieted down with the attention being focused on the man who spoke.

"Thank you," he said.

The plainness and sincerity with which it was said were like nothing I had ever experienced. For the first time in a long time, I couldn't help but feel the emotion of the moment and I could sense a tear roll down my own cheek. I quickly rubbed the evidence from my face, but it was to no avail. When I looked around, almost everyone was emotionally distraught.

With that, the field workers we had rescued, except Foggdog, all made their way out of the control room to share the good news with the thousands still waiting for confirmation of their liberation.

In the meantime, my attention turned to the guards who were now all sitting against the wall – prisoners to whatever we had in store for them. I quickly adjusted my attitude from glorious victor to ruthless prison warden. I walked the line in front of where they sat, acting all the part of a leader of a riotous band of militiamen who had just stormed their compound and taken control.

I said nothing, just stared at their faces. All of them seemed frightened; and I could almost feel a sense of guilt emanating from each of them for what they had done. I remembered what Art had told us about the men not being trained guards, but being thrust into this role as the situation called for it.

And in the back of my mind I kept thinking of that electric car. That car would show up tomorrow, and if everything didn't seem as though it were normal, then we might have a heavy faction of the American military at our front doorstep, and all this could be for naught.

"Gentlemen," I said. "You have a lot of atonement to do."

That didn't seem to ease their discomfort.

"Over the last few months, you have been running a forced labor camp here, in the *United States of America*. People are hungry, people are overworked and you have broken your promises."

I kept walking the line, back and forth, pacing during the moments I chose not to speak. I must say, I was appropriately dramatic and I could tell it was having an effect on our new prisoners. In the moments between making statements, I could feel the stress of our prisoners rising as they questioned, *"What are you going to do to us?"*

"The people out in those tents," I continued. "They are my friends, my neighbors. You promised them food and security, and you gave them neither. And that is why we have come."

Expecting them to show some sign of anger or resistance, I continued to pace. Their compound had been stormed and they had been taken prisoner, yet there seemed almost an air of acceptance of every word I said and every action I took. No resistance came.

I looked behind me and saw the whole team standing there, as if they were waiting for me to figure out what to do next. But I was confident that what I was about to do was right. I remembered Sun Tzu:

"The best policy is to capture the state intact; it should be destroyed only if no other options are available."

At that moment, the lights flickered back on and the computers began whirring. Steven had successfully repaired the electricity.

I turned back to our prisoners. "Gentlemen," I said. "You are very lucky today. You are lucky that we are the ones who decided to take over your little camp here. See, we don't want any more trouble – we just want our friends and neighbors to be free."

There seemed to be an air of relief among them once I said that.

"From now on, the comings and goings of the people in this compound will be overseen by us. Farming, work schedules, food distribution, access to and from the camp will be regulated by us," I said, continuing to pace in front of the men. There was no protest from the former guards.

"However," I said. "I know that you have been placed in a tough position. You are clearly not military, yet you carry guns and try to impose your will. For that and for the things you have done, you will have to answer to your own conscience."

I kept walking the line, every step echoing in the large chamber.

"What were we supposed to do?" questioned an indiscernible voice from within the line.

I stopped cold and then turned to face them. "What were you supposed to do?" I asked, more than slightly aggravated. "You were supposed to treat people as you would have wanted to be treated yourself. You were supposed to be humane – to take people in from the cold and to offer the people the option to work to fulfill their needs rather than demanding it at the point of a gun!"

The room went quiet again. The guards knew they were wrong. I could see it in their faces – some strewn with tears now that they were on the opposite end of torment. I wanted to make sure that this threat soaked into their brains, but I also knew that the power had been out and the communications lines had been down for at least twenty minutes now. Maybe somebody somewhere would be missing them. I needed to get them back in their chairs with a willingness to do the jobs they had always done.

"I am not a terrorist," I exclaimed. "Nor am I a tormentor or torturer. My men here will begin to question each of you as to your role in this compound and how it relates to whoever it is on the other end of those phone lines and whoever it is who shows up every day in that electric car. Can we do that?"

There was no answer.

I took an audibly deep breath and then asked again, as if appalled they wouldn't agree with this deal at the first offer. "Can we do that?"

A man in from the far end of the line stood up slowly and quietly with his hands raised in the air. He seemed to be a little older than me, perhaps in his mid-40's, clean-shaven and seemingly in good shape. Perhaps he was the senior member of the guards. "Excuse me, sir," he politely interrupted.

I walked over to him briskly. "Yes?" I asked.

"Is this... *all* that you ask of us?" as if he expected there to be more.

"Yes," I answered. "Yes, it is."

His head looked straight down to the ground and he began to cry, apparently in shame for the way he had treated my neighbors and friends. His voice wavered and he never answered yes or no, instead offering something else rather unexpected.

"Thank you," he said. "Thank you, sir."

Then, to a man, the guards stood up one at a time, and nodded their heads. "Thank you, sir," the first one said. "Thank you, sir," the next. And the next, and the next, and the next, right down the line.

They had never asked for their role in the first place. It had come to them with no option and their wills were not strong enough to make the right choice. They had done what they were told to do, perhaps knowing that if they weren't on the back-end of that gun, they would likely be on the front-end of one in a labor camp somewhere else. Perhaps it wasn't the proper choice in terms of being the right thing to do, but it may have been the option with the greatest chance of survival. Now, not only were they getting off scot-free for their poor-decisions and egregious actions, but they were going to be on the good guys' team. And for that, they were thankful.

I nodded in approval, and then walked over to Ed Marino and Hank. "Get them up and running the computers again. Make sure they don't send out any sort of distress call and keep them in our good graces. I think we're going to be in good shape here."

Mitch and Foggdog stood in front of the door, neither of them doing a good job at withholding the smiles on their faces.

"We did it," Mitch said.

"We did," I acknowledged.

"I just have one question," Foggdog admitted.

"What's that?"

"What did you mean when you said you thought that noise was my girlfriend?"

I had almost forgotten, and it caused me to laugh. And just at that moment, the front door opened and in ran our sniper, dropping her weapon lightly to the ground and embracing her boyfriend Foggdog... who from then on lost the nickname and was only known as she would know him – "Jimmy."

As they embraced in a happy reunion, I decided turn my attention back outside. Leaving our prisoners in good hands, I made my way to the camp to check on my old neighbors and friends. I had no idea what to expect when I opened the door, but what I saw overwhelmed me beyond comprehension. Every man, woman and child who resided in the camp stood before me. For the briefest moment, there was pure silence. And then the clapping started. It was very light at first, and then a little more and a little more. It built up quickly to a crescendo, complete with whistles and screams of joy.

Looking at their faces, I realized that I had never known the feeling of true appreciation before. I looked back through the open door behind me and could see the men smiling, remembering the reason we did all this in the first place. I thought of all the years of my life I spent sitting in the office and how every day during that time paled in comparison to what I had done today. Today, I had truly made a difference and done something that I'd never be able to do from behind a corporate desk in some cubicle. I finally allowed myself to relinquish the role of militia leader and accept the role of caring neighbor. As emotion overwhelmed me, the crowd mobbed me with hugs and thanks – random women, young and old, even the occasional man kissing me on the cheek or the head.

They were just happy to be free and I was happy we could give that to them. As I waded through the crowd, an occasional familiar face said hello, but none was as grateful as that of Mrs. Quigley.

"Thank you," she said. "I can't believe you are here. Thank you!"

"Mrs. Quigley," I said. "You have no idea what your gift, that little key, meant to this effort. Without that key, we very well might not have made it here today."

She smiled coyly, as if unwittingly accepting some role in her own liberation – a role she most certainly deserved.

I found a tree stump among the tents and stepped up on it to address the crowd. As soon as I steadied myself upon the stump and faced them, a hush quickly silenced the whole place.

"Friends and neighbors," I began. "We have come here to liberate you." I actually had more to say in that sentence, but everyone erupted in applause, which lasted a bit long and I had to hush them back to silence before continuing.

"Unfortunately, the messenger you sent us, Art Brady, passed away shortly after delivering his message." There was a noticeable sigh among the crowd, and though Art certainly deserved recognition for his part in all of this, I didn't want to dwell on the past. There was too much to do still. "We do not have fuel, nor do we have ample food supplies. But what we do have is this land and our hard work and a renewed sense of responsibility for each other. Tomorrow, we will begin again. Tomorrow, we will make sure that all of you have some role to play in the resurrection of this community. Celebrate tonight, for you will no longer be required to work at the point of a gun. But come tomorrow, we enter a new era – one where we work hard to provide for each other. This is just the beginning. Now that you've paid the price of not having freedom, tomorrow you will carry the burden of being free."

That was all I needed to say, so I stepped off the stump amidst the crowd. You could tell they wanted to be jovial and celebrate, but the truth was that they were not going to wake up tomorrow in some sort of paradise. Things weren't magically going to go back to the way they were.

This was a rescue from tyranny, but I had no immediate solutions or abundance of resources. All I had was the promise of freedom. They would have to help do the rest.

I made my way back into the main building where the mood was a little more relaxed this time. The guards were sitting at their stations. Mitch, Hank, and Ed Marino were leading the effort, keeping an eye on them to make sure they stayed in line, which seemed to be the case. They almost seemed anxious to be working for us, rather than those on the other end of the phones. There was a bigger sense of purpose now.

I was itching to get back to the house and tell Charlotte and Anna the good news, but I needed to make sure things had settled here before I went back.

Ed sensed my anxiety.

"I'd say you'd earned an early leave here, today," he said.

I smiled, realizing that of course they would know what was on my mind at that point.

"We've got this taken care of."

And they did. I knew they did. I had never asked for the supervisor's role in all of this. It had just somehow found its way to me. On the one hand, I felt the burden of responsibility to now run the camp and see that it was restored in a good and fair manner. But on the other hand, I desperately wanted to go home to my family. When I looked around, I saw my friends working diligently – Mitch, Jimmy, the Marinos, Colin, Pete, Hank, Steven, and the rest of the men. I knew they had it all under control and I was no longer needed. At least not tonight – not when a woman and her little girl waited nervously for news from the battlefront.

So I headed out to my truck, still parked out by the main building garage, and went home.

CHAPTER TWENTY-FOUR

As the truck ascended the hill, the big oak tree slowly revealed itself and I knew that I was finally home. Pulling into the driveway, the engine coughed a bit and then cut off completely as the truck coasted to a stop right in front of the garage. Just enough gas to make it home.

I unplugged my phone from the charger and put the wire back into the glove compartment where I had always kept it. I was tempted to turn it on, but resisted.

The front door to the house swung open and the two most beautiful women in the world ran out to greet me. I don't know if you can call it a reunion if you had just seen each other that same morning, but it sure felt like one. We embraced for quite a while next to the truck in the warm evening air.

Always thinking of others, Charlotte's first question was, "Is everyone ok?"

"Yes. It went just as planned and everyone is ok. Not as much as a sprained toe. There was only one shot fired the whole time."

"Let me guess," Charlotte said. "One of those crazy guys with the machine gun?"

"Good guess," I answered. Of course, the truth would have probably been her *last* guess. "Believe it or not, it was Katie."

Charlotte cricked her head, as if startled by that revelation.

"Come on, let's go inside," I said. "I'll tell you all about it."

"We have a surprise for you, Dad," Anna added with a sly grin. "Come in, come in."

Draping my arm around my wife's shoulder, the two of us followed our daughter into the kitchen. Inside, the table was nicely set with candles lit and a centerpiece of newly-picked tulips. An inviting smell emanated from some unidentifiable place where food had been cooking.

"What is *that*?" I asked as I sniffed the air wanting to inhale as much of the pleasant aroma as I could.

"You came at exactly the right time," Charlotte said. "We just finished."

Removing the cover off a platter on the table, she revealed the most amazing meal, highlighted by large, juicy pork chops. The only meat we had eaten since the power had gone out was the game we trapped, or the little bits in canned soups and hashes we had in our stores.

"Where in the world did you get this?" I asked.

"Ed Marino's pig," she answered. "Remember?"

"But…"

"It was in the basket, under the bacon," she said, as she started serving the meat. The smell was simply unrelenting, and my eyes rolled back in my head in anticipation. "Here," said Charlotte, handing over a handwritten note that was also inside the basket.

It was short and sweet:

Charlotte,
Please accept this as a gift. Your husband will be hungry when he comes home this evening.
Ed Marino

Charlotte placed her hand on my face and stared into my eyes. It must have been hell not knowing whether she'd be eating this wonderful meal with me or perhaps with Katie Marino. I'm not sure much of the food in front of us would have actually been eaten if that were the case.

"I'm so glad you're home," she said softly.

"Me too, Daddy," Anna chimed in.

For too many times in one day, a tear ran down my cheek. "I am too," I echoed. "I am too."

The meal tasted as good as it looked, though my mouth was often too busy chatting, reliving the day's events. Dinner lasted quite a while – I guess we were just happy that this day had come and gone about as successfully as it could possibly go and didn't want the moment to end.

"And guess who says 'hello'?" I asked Anna.

"Who?" she wondered.

"Mrs. Quigley."

"Really?" she asked. "Will we be able to see her at the library again soon?"

"I hope so, sweetie," I said. "I hope so."

We ate and we talked and at some moments we even laughed. Shortly after dinner, Anna fell asleep – I guess it was as long a day for her as it was for us. I carried her up to bed, laid her down and kissed her goodnight. I took a moment to look at her and hope that my actions on this day would only help her see better opportunity in the future. Then I went back downstairs where Charlotte sat in front of the fireplace with two glasses of red wine.

"Where'd you get those?" I asked.

"I hid a bottle a few months ago," she said. "I figured that if it was the last bottle on Earth, maybe I should keep it for a more appropriate time. Tonight seemed appropriate."

"It sure does," I agreed, and sat next to her on the couch. Picking up the wine, we said "Cheers!" and clanked glasses.

"To freedom," she said.

"To freedom."

I never remembered wine tasting so good.

"I have a present for you, too," I said.

"Oh really?"

"Yes," I said, and retrieved my cell phone from my pocket. "Ever since Art arrived here that night, I have been trying to justify risking my life for the freedom of others who voluntarily placed themselves in their own oppressive predicament. Things just slowly moved me towards that direction – gathering the weapons, running into Colin, and Jimmy getting captured. But I still needed something more," I admitted, tapping the phone's screen with my index finger. "And then I realized there was something even bigger than all that. In the end, do you know what it really was that I was fighting for?"

"What?" she asked.

I turned on the phone and the screen came alive, revealing the picture of Anna in her sneakers, standing in the puddle next to the library with the beautiful rainbow streaking across the background sky. The smile on her face was so pure and innocent and in that moment she represented everything a child her age should have – freedom, security, opportunity, happiness.

I took a deep breath and showed Charlotte the picture.

"I'm pretty sure it was this."

ABOUT THE AUTHOR

Liberty Gulch is A.G. Fredericks' second novel. His first novel, The Troy Standard, was also self-published and widely acclaimed. A.G. lives with his wife and daughter in Western Massachusetts.

Made in the USA
San Bernardino, CA
17 August 2013